Lipstick and Other Stories

Books by Alex Kuo

The Window Tree
New Letters from Hiroshima
Changing the River
Chinese Opera
This Fierce Geography

Lipstick and Other Stories

Alex Kuo

An Orchid Pavilion Book
Asia 2000 Limited
Hong Kong

ISBN: 962-7160-99-7

Published by Asia 2000 Ltd
15 B, 263 Hollywood Road,
Sheung Wan, Hong Kong

http://www.asia2000.com.hk

Typeset in Adobe Garamond by Kashif Akhtar, Asia 2000 Ltd
Printed in Hong Kong by Editions Quaille

First Printing 2001
Second Printing 2002

For my seniors at Beijing Forestry University, 1990
who gave me these stories the hard way,

and for Joan and Sara
who listened to them and kept them going.

Grateful acknowledgement is extended to the editors of the following publications in which some of these stories first appeared, sometimes in earlier versions: "The Peking Cowboy" in *Blue Mesa Review;* "Smoke" and "Morning Stars" in *Caliban;* "Eggs," "Absences," "Growing Tomatoes," and "Cicadas" in *Chicago Review;* "The Catholic All-Star Chess Team" in *dimsum;* "Reductions" in *Ergo!;* "Definitions" in *Green Mountains Review;* "Reductions" in *New Orleans Review;* "Lipstick" in *Ploughshares;* "Definition" in *Portland Review;* "Family Stories," "Relocation," "Past Perfect Tense," and "The Catholic All-Star Chess Team" in *The Redneck Review of Literature;* "Exit, a Chinese Novel" in *Universe;* and "The Connoisseur of Chaos" in *Charlie Chan is Dead,* edited by Jessica Hagedorn.

Contents

Contents

SECTION III

Lipstick and Other Stories

Section I

Section 1

Eggs

When they were children, both my grandmothers had their feet bound; thereafter they had to learn to balance their feelings very carefully. *The pain too will pass,* Renoir had said in 1903. Renoir was to become a friend of my mother Katherine who was not yet born at the time he first said these words; but he repeated every word in 1910 when she was two and they became friends. This time however, he was not referring to the pain which accompanied Katherine's mother's bound feet when she was a child, but instead anticipated the alienation that Katherine was to later feel from the Tai Chung community for not binding her feet. Strangers sitting on the stoops of their houses and shops all over the city would point to her outsized feet and untethered walk and whisper comments under their breath.

—

At five Katherine said to Renoir, I will never drop an egg from the high beam.

—

Later she went to school abroad and met her husband shortly after he had publicly cut his cue during a Berkeley demonstration.

Then the magical happened in 1914 in Chongqing; overnight, Katherine disappeared from our lives, followed by absolute silence. For the first forty-three years after her disappearance, not a whisper was said in the family about Katherine or her disappearance, at least not within my listening.

—

But now the children and the other children are beginning to dissent. First there was the memory that would not go away. Then there was the garrulous word *Renoir,* eventually hatching questions. Then the whispers ripped up the shaded heart. Soon the nights were humming with telephone conversations. We made contact with the secretary of immigration, the archivist of birth records, the alumni minister; we poured over maps and old driving records; we interviewed postal carriers, tricksters, insurance chancellors, and even tried to get into the Mormon Redemption Center. We looked up every taxonomy and geography, and collected everything tangible from both sides of the Pacific.

—

We are here for the duration, carefully balanced between address and rumor, carefully watching those who are siphoning from our pain, allowing us to go on.

—

In the early morning our children will thrust from our thighs and float away from us, like chilled stars.

Absences

In the early spring of 1944, the Yangtze River wrecked its annual havoc on the inhabitants living along its shores. I had turned five, and remember crossing the river with my parents at the height of its flood.

No. In 1944 I crossed the Yangtze River with my parents. It appeared to me as a five-year old that most of the world had sunk under the turbulent heavy water. There as flotsam, the branches and logs and pieces of lumber, a dead chicken, bloated goat, carried a sucking dark smell that the wind and brown current would not dissipate.

—

Everything has shifted just a little since, probably including more of what wasn't there than what was.

—

From the first tense of my memory life, I have only two or three impressions of my father. This was one of them. He seldom told by example, and even less by word. He was away most of the time, but he was to tell me four years later when I had just finished practicing the piano, he said, *Don't follow in the steps of Turgenev.*

So this one I remember, though not in this order. The Yangtze starts somewhere in the Tibetan Highlands and meanders some 3,500 miles before it empties into the East China Sea at Shanghai. Until dams and levees were constructed to control the river's annual spring flood, much of the lowlands was threatened every year. But this was 1944, years before the completion of the flood-control project.

The water was muddy that spring; that is to say, I remember the color of the water.

—

Shouting at another boat that had turned over upstream from ours, our boatman steered to scavenge the planking drifting downriver from the fast sinking sampan. From the opposite end of ours, my father stood up dangerously with an oar and threatened to knock him overboard unless he helped the drowning victims of the overturned boat. It had taken courage for me to get into that little boat in that swift water in the first place; then I cried and shivered and held onto my mother's hand for comfort, and kept an anxious eye on the diminishing, closest shore. But the voices of my father's and the boatman's — shouting, cursing, threatening — made the crest of the opposite shore tilt ever so steeper as the two of them pitched back and forth, both boats sweeping downriver out of control.

—

High above the Yangtze that summer, we lived in a house on a plateau to the south of the river. It was the last summer that my brother Will lived at home, and the last summer that our father had a garden for his tomatoes. It was also the year before the end of the war.

—

If what happened imperfectly there on that river included my holding onto my mother Katherine's hand for the crossing, I have no image of her face, not even from earlier photographs. I held onto her same hand again a year later when she and I flew from Chongqing to Shanghai in a stuffed C-47 cargo plane with makeshift wooden seats roped along its inside wall.

—

It was also a summer that involved a strange funeral procession that left me stranded by the gates of the house. Was it my mother's, or was it someone else's hand that I held onto during the flight to Shanghai? Did Katherine disappear that summer, or the next?

—

Now when I am alone playing a piece on the piano, I sometimes hear the pitch shifting ever so slightly above the noise of that summer. Under my eyelids I can still see the pagodas perched high in the distance above the gorge of that rampaging river in my sleep, the tiny monks sequestered from the roily din below.

Growing Tomatoes

In 1944 when I was very young, my family lived in a huge house outside Chongqing, just a stone's throw from the river that flooded every spring. We had goats, ducks and geese that chased after me, and a vegetable garden. I remember my father gathering giant tomatoes from his garden and juicing them into a large porcelain bowl on the square dining room table. I still remember the glassfuls tasting dank and dark. To this day I still cannot stand its rawness, but drink it camouflaged in a Bloody Mary.

Since I've moved to Idaho and live in my own house, I've been raising vegetable gardens in the backyard every season. Among the corn, squash, eggplant, spinach and beet I've always saved room for a few tomato plants, even though I never eat them but give them away to friends at harvest time.

In the middle of the summer I sometimes walk out of the house and listen to these plants grow, often flicking tiny black aphids from off their stems and leaves. In these moments the tangy odor of their leaves draw childhood recollections of a father dead nineteen years, images of his hands immersed in the white porcelain bowl of tomato juice from his garden, him saying *Drink it, drink it, it's only good for you, it's vitamin C.*

Tonight, at exactly my father's age in 1944 and nearly five thousand miles and fifty years from my past, I wake to hear the tomato leaves brushing gently against the backdoor of my house in the breeze, and soon after, the fruit bursting like blood in the burgeoning quarter moon.

Cicadas

This happened in 1944, probably well into summer, at least several months after the Yangtze had receded. The war must have started turning around for Chiang Kaishek; past the heavy wooden gates of our villa, endless columns of Kuomintang troops were daily marching towards the coast on the road parallel to the river. Breaking the monotonous clanging of their mess kits, stirred the occasional low whirring hum of a staff car with its unit chevron, or a truck, its canvas flap concealing what was inside. But mostly there were hundreds and hundreds of soldiers moving at the same speed as the vehicles, their uniform the exact ordinary color as the road dust they stirred. Some of them didn't have rifles, and I remember my brother Will saying that some of the others did not have ammunition. One or two of these faces would always be turned up towards where I was watching them from the top step in front of the gates. My mother told me I had to keep the gates closed. I was five that summer, and lowered the bar on the gates as I was told.

That was also the summer I learned about cicadas and departures of another kind. Will had a highly prized bamboo stick at least twelve or fifteen feet long, and he taught me how to catch cicadas with it. First he would show me by example, then he would stand behind me and help me as I was tested before I was on my own, even when he wasn't watching.

We would first slowly twist the upper tip of the stick around spider webs in crevices around the house and the wall that surrounded the house until the tip was crested and darkened with the sticky cobweb. When he was helping me, there were four hands on the stick turning it in unison, and I remember feeling a sense of purposefulness in that exactitude. Occasionally he would ask me to let go of the stick so that he could reach higher under the roof's edges.

Finding the cicadas was easy. We stood still and listened. It seemed in that summer the steady stridulation of a high pitched resonance was always in the air. Even today when every other noise is down in my life, my inner ear can echo that continuous sound, the electrical strike of cicadas at first hearing. We listened for breaks in that sound, a short but sustained grinding note repeated again and again, and followed it to the small darkish lumps on tree branches silhouetted against the clear skies of Chongqing.

The delicate movement of approaching the cicadas from below and behind was the most difficult technique to learn. It had to be done slowly, so the insect would not be frightened off, but not so slowly to allow its escape. I now suspect the truthfulness of this part of Will's instruction as much as his report about the soldiers' ammunition supply. Once I mustered enough strength to control the quivering of the stick's tip fifteen feet up and made contact, the cicada was doomed.

What I don't remember now is what we did with the cicadas afterwards. I imagine that Will probably had a little stick cage for them, or a matchbox, in which he kept alive our collection with daily ablutions of water. We would lift it once in a while, shake it, expecting to stimulate ethereal song from the captured cicadas.

This was the summer of my earliest recollection; and it has been held captive until now in these unspoken and inescapable images. This was also the summer during which Will, being married at the time, had slipped into the bed of a servant one night and was henceforth banished forever into a cage of his own making.

Past Perfect Tense

It happened when I wasn't paying any attention to the particulars. Perhaps too young then, in a village outside Chongqing along the Yangtze in 1944, I was awed more by the soldiers whose columns marched by our house, keeping ahead of each other, Chiang Kaishek's troops corrupted and tousled, Mao Zedong's spoiling for a repetition, and the Imperial Japanese Army's looking for any shelter, however merciful. Overhead the mercenary Flying Tigers flew their fattened C-46s east over the Hump with munitions and filing cabinets, and returned with Steinway CDs and the DPs who could afford this necessity in gold.

It is difficult now to imagine that I was in the middle of events that changed the lives of close to one billion people; but to a child, their significance held no portent. Surely the sunlight must have moved shadows behind trees and buildings that autumn, and just as surely someone must have recorded that moment in a journal. But what happened in fact in one short moment that fall afternoon some forty-four years and five thousand miles from the here and now — the single event that must have touched thousands, however catastrophic, ordinary or benign, its continuum breaking down into disconnected fragments, each with its own urgent tedium to attend to — has escaped history, its memory privileged and wordless.

So there in that afternoon sunlight, holding onto my mother's hand on the way to the airport to catch the last flight out to Shanghai in a C-46 jammed with chickens, smuggled gold and political DPs staying ahead of Mao's troops, saying goodbye to my dog and my father, who was to join us later, I asked my father what would happen to my dog that was to be left behind. A behaviorist who believed in telling selected truths to his children, Zing Yang said *Someone will probably catch it and eat it.* After the war, neither one of us was to mention this episode again for the rest of his life.

—

After the war, curled up in its darkest tense, only the memory has stirred, afraid to wake up. But since memory is also inventive, it can now realign what has happened in that one moment in the past and allow me to walk away from its significant rubble. It is a prodigal hand forever reaching out, mending. That is the story that has been left behind.

—

In my dream last night, I was taking a walk in the hollowed braces of my house where all life began. Sunlight filtered through the intricate and warmed all possibilities. I was singing the story of a silver trout returned from the seas. I had heard it the day before from a Chilean woman who had escaped gravity and become the justice that we all want. There was no hunger, drought or pestilence.

A cinnamon bear cub attached itself to my back, a supple pinioning ready for play. We wrestled, feigned in the air's magnitude, bristly fur and skin swamped in perfect ferociousness until I had to leave. But the cub would not let go. I reasoned that I could not raise a bear in the city, the neighborhood covenants would be challenged, the SPCA would be inspecting its diet, exercise and socialization, and I would have to leave it alone for long periods. Still the bear would not let go, and tightened its story around my shoulders, until it suddenly let go completely and fell just after the exploding BANG BANG came from the edge of the house. A hunter stood there with his red cap and rifle, a hunting license pasted to the white bones of his face.

Most of the time I don't hear it, but this time I heard myself yell *It isn't necessary, It isn't necessary* until the roar took me out of my dream, lest I forget it had ever happened.

Relocation After The Manhattan Project

Everybody who goes there will go crazy
— Leo Szilard, 1942

In 1942 my mother and I had just moved to Chongqing into the middle of the wars. On its return flight to Hong Kong, the converted C-46 carried escaping displaced persons who had slivered gold pieces up in their vaginas and anuses. At that precise moment when chaos yields exactly to chaos in my memory, my mother died, cause unknown.

This was a story I had no words for.

This was a story that had existed only at the edge.

For my distancing, I have kept my house very clean. When I answer students looking for ways around suicide, I am careful to fold these words over my own throat, *I know, I know, I know, I know,* everything else becoming pale — the flooding Yangtze, sheer wind at Chongqing airport, cicada cages, dank-tasting tomato juice, the mysterious funeral — as if none of it had ever happened, in metaphor or translation.

—

These numbers appear suddenly on my computer screen. There are 263 warheads targeted for every Soviet community over 100,000: Hartford, Springfield, Cedar Rapids, Milwaukee, Providence, Boulder, Spokane, Boise, Salt Lake City. There are 3.2 tons of TNT deposited in the World Bank for every person on earth.

—

I come into my story now, just as you are, on the eve of my return. There is much to be accounted for, Ilse Koch and her Buchenwald roses, Captain Jack, Hiroshima, Los Alamos; it is my reason for getting up in the mornings. What is the Chinese word for this mending?

—

Last week I found a silver trout washed ashore in a stream not far from the back of the house, its eyes closed against the coming freeze. Its mouth held a letter my mother wrote just before she died. In it she said to a friend, *Trust me, Trust me, never forget where the heart begins.* Taking the edge out of the fold, I carefully replaced the letter and nudged the fish down into the water. In a moment, it transformed itself into a crane that disappeared into my heart, welling a small crucible of warmth forever.

Family Stories

I was carrying two potatoes
a woman came up
She wanted to buy the two potatoes
she had children
I did not give her the two potatoes
I hid the two potatoes
I had a mother.

— Anna Swirszczynska, 1944

There was a moment during the war, in 1942, that telling the story accurately and truthfully was less compelling for my mother Kitty than our survival of the story unfolding about us. Travelling on a military passport with me to Chongqing to meet her husband and my father, after crossing North America from Boston to Vancouver by rail and the Pacific by commercial flight to Hong Kong, and then Shanghai, she had to wait days for an irregular military transport for the final 1,500 miles of the journey.

In 1942, Shanghai was a city under siege, the massive panic for once breaking down the racist barriers of its foreign settlements and concessions. The sky had disappeared entirely for its residents, and the random acts of individuals swelled in conspicuous violence and exploitation, shrilled, roared, and, hooved in scaffold, everywhere ran, crowding, day and night. Lives fermented in essential lies and contingency lies, ideology and metaphor abandoned, huddled around betrayal and survival, sucking.

It must have happened in a moment when my mother wasn't paying constant attention to her three-year-old son. I was stolen, grabbed from my mother's side while she had slipped momentarily into an exhausted sleep. When she woke up and discovered I was missing, and recognized it for what it meant in that city at that time, she must have cursed and yelled breathless and silent in her grieved determination. To keep her consciousness from falling apart, it took all her will and all of her family's money to find me and ransom me back into her story, but not before one of my abductors had spilled scalding water onto my left thigh, leaving a scar for life.

After this incident my mother changed her name and went underground. She did not take a military C-46 or C-47 to Chongqing along with escaping DPs and Madame Chiang Kaishek's Steinway CD. We traveled at night, rode in vegetable carts, taking chunks out of the 1,500 miles that followed the Yangtze River to Chongqing. During the day we sought shelter in monasteries and caves, evading the soldiers on constant march on that singular narrow road edged high into the gorge over the green shallows of the river. Even at night we avoided the civilians rich enough to have a reason to go somewhere.

At Chongqing we had to wait for months before my father arrived. We lived in a cave and ate what we could find; this same woman who less than a year ago had left me in a nursery in Milton Hospital on Sunday afternoons to go sailing in Hingham Bay or dinner at the best upstairs table in the Ritz where everyone kowtowed to her, now spread rugs to stay off the ground's dampness.

But it was not enough to keep the humidity from her lungs, and later pneumonia, which lingered until it turned into tuberculosis from which she died a few short months later, high on a bluff overlooking the Yangtze after its seasonal flooding.

The rest of us survived the war. In reconstructing new lives and making things normal again, my father Zing Yang conspired to keep her story from me, since it was not exactly a history that any-one would want to recall in a post-war random dinner conversa-tion. But last week a friend of Kitty's who still lives in Massachu-setts, found me by phone in my office, and called wanting to let me know all of it before she turned 80 and started blurring the details.

Having survived both, I find a half century later that I had a mother whose story I can now begin to know. I have kept the name on my birth certificate over these years; they will keep their real names in these stories, because they were not innocent — I know this is true, this is fiction. As I insert these closing words I want to say that I would like to stay in one place long enough to explain to my children what has happened, until that echo comes back and embraces us in the retelling, but I'm not sure it will hap-pen here.

Section II

Bloodline

My stepmother never married my father after my mother died. "We were the only ones left" in the middle of the war, she told me when I asked over the phone forty-five years later, "and started to live together for survival. We were the only ones left."

Later she wrote "I regret you didn't ask your dad while he was still around" what happened to my mother. "As far as I can recall, your mom was a pretty tall woman, not at all talkative. At least she and I seldom talked. I wasn't the physician in charge. I was in bed myself with a high fever."

—

Two years later she wrote again, "My friends tell me you are going to China to teach linguistics. Why haven't you told me? Will you be teaching in Chinese?"

And then another letter waiting for me when I arrived asked "What is linguistics? Does the AMA approve of it? Have you regained your proficiency in speaking Chinese, especially Mandarin? I thank God my days are quite filled."

When my sister and I were still living at home, she would speak to us only in Chinese while she spoke English to everyone else she knew, even when the only words they understood were *okay, bye-*

bye and *fuck*. Now she speaks to me and Xiaomi in English only, that is, when she speaks to her at all, even though they live only blocks apart in the same zip code.

—

One early Sunday morning after Xiaomi had a near fatal accident driving on the LA freeways by herself, her mother called. "You're her brother," she announced. "Tell her to never ever drive again."

Ten minutes after we hung up, Xiaomi called and wanted to know what I was doing on the phone at three in the morning in China. "How can I convince Mother not to leave any more birds' nest soup on my doorstep in the middle of the night when I'm asleep? Doesn't she know it's not FDA approved?"

I pretended to understand what she'd said but reminded her she had left ducks and once a swan that had wandered in range of her errant fowling piece, on her mother's doorsteps after a weekend of hunting in District Ten.

Over the years they have also traded kittens without consent or acknowledgment.

—

After I'd been here a month teaching linguistic theory, my step-mother called again at two in the morning.

"You wrote if you should take the typhoid shot."

"That's good, mother. You called to tell me that? D'you know what time it is here?"

"Yes, yes. It's only a rumor. It's not useful. There's plenty of time for diagnosis and treatment; there's no need for any gene-tricking immunization, not even the oral type."

Since it was her nickel, I couldn't resist asking how Xiaomi was recovering from her accident and if the birds' nest soup was working.

"Xiaomi phoned me this evening telling me she saw you off in San Francisco. I'm sorry she didn't let me know, otherwise I could at least see you two for a moment at the airport. Maybe she would let me know when you return. If I am still around by then."

I took a deep suck on a cigarette and stared hard into the black phone in my hand.

—

She called again at the same time the next morning.

"Mother, who's paying for these trans-Pacific calls?"

"Medicare."

"Right. How're you doing mother?'

I was encouraged. I remembered one early summer when I was twelve and my softball team was practicing minus its shortstop because for three months I was home learning to type by transcribing my father's autobiography, *Confessions of a Chinese Scientist*. Today I don't remember anything of what was in it and even the title's unreliable. But I struggled and eventually learned to decipher his handwriting.

"Fine. The photo you sent standing in front of Genghis Khan's birth yurt when you went to Hohhot — you are wrong! You are believing too many commercials again. Look closely. There are wheels under the yurt. It's off a movie set."

His manuscript was never published, and that season I lost my only chance at shortstop but ended up catcher for the rest of my softball career because no one else wanted to wear the mask.

—

The phone was ringing when I came back to my apartment from my morning lecture. I hesitated at first, but I picked it up.

"Your companion just called and said she felt you had slipped off earth's edge. She misses you, but doesn't know exactly what she is missing since everything seems too unreal."

"You're lying mother. She's never met you, and it's midnight your time."

There were starlings on the telephone wire outside my window this time. I could hear us talking away over the little echoes of distraction.

—

I did not bury my mother; I wasn't old enough to force them. I waited for her to come back, three years, ten years, and forty. I don't believe she's gone, and do. I'm not ten-years-old anymore. My body knows — it roils just above the deepest silence and the most steadfast family distance.

The Peking Cowboy

It didn't feel right; he held the six-point elk in the crosshairs of his Leupold 3 x 9, but it didn't feel right. He wanted to know, he wanted to know now in these aspens of another high October tucked away in the divide between the St. Joe and Clearwater's North Fork. So while the bull humped its escape into another drainage, he slipped his rifle into its scabbard, jumped on his mare and squeezed her from Bad Assed Ridge down the veloured slopes to the corral-camp by his pickup bound for the nearest Chinese restaurant in Moscow.

Past the swinging half-doors of the Peking in his muddy boots he asked the waitress for a fortune cookie.

"You can't have one until you've had a meal here," the waitress with the dark lips and serious ways said.

"But I'm not hungry." Impatience was growing, he needed to know without another moment's interference.

"There is another way, but you already know that, don't you? You'll have to tell me a story first, and you must tell it to me truthfully and without changing a word of it."

His will conceding its pulse to this substitute mandate, the two of them got into his pickup for the return drive to his camp.

They both knew the ritual well in this scheherazade. At the corral she saddled up the blue roan and rode up to the lean-to by the side of a cirque. While he tended to the horses, she started a small

45

fire with the toothpicks and credit card slips she had pocketed on their way out of the restaurant. Then they sat down on rocks opposite each other, the fire between them ringed, a sliver of day-moon rising over the ridge beside them, his loaded rifle by his side.

While her attention drifted away into a shadow, he started the story very cautiously. "It is early autumn, and the morning sunlight shines through the window onto my opened copy of *Vanity Fair* in front of me." He knew it was not his story, but he felt he was the story's in which its space and order took over. He wanted to tell the story in the third person, but it came out in the first; he wanted to tell it in the past, but it came out happening in the now; even if he wanted to, he could not change a word of it, its sequence and language clarifying its own shape and direction in his voice.

During this short pause she looked over to him and said, "Careful now, you know what you must do," but it was as much a self-reminder as a warning.

So he continued. "The visiting foreign expert is a literary scholar from the University of London who will direct our graduate seminar for the year, but he can see that I am the only student who is not taking notes on his Thackeray lecture. He continues to call me by *Daniel,* a name given to me by my first-year English teacher at this language institute a few years ago, instead of *Luojun.*" He stopped here to check the authenticity of this identity. The waitress looked up from the fire too, but didn't say a thing. So he continued. "But the two of us have an understanding, even though we do not trust each other.

"It is the fourth week of class, and he has not called on me since I asked him during our first meeting if there is any significance that nine of the ten authors in this novel course are British, the tenth being Henry James, and that all ten were published before the twentieth century. He reminds me of our cadre leader, a party member who conducted our ideology studies every day in middle school. But the professor tries to be different, and introduces a small joke in Chinese in the middle of every lecture, about his minor bicycle collision in downtown Beijing, about being cheated buying fruit at the open market, after which we all smile politely."

Adding sticks to the receding fire, the waitress leaned down and blew some air to revive its flame while the cowboy took a drink of water from his canteen thermos.

"One of my brothers still sells fruit at the open market every morning, as all the children in the family have at some time since our father died. So I look away from his joke and see the wall around this new department building, and the wall around the entire institute and at all the walls in and around Beijing. Before I was born my parents farmed this land that is now the campus, as did their parents and their parents before them when they were not servants to the emperor or empress, like everybody else in Peking who were not members of the burgeoning bureaucracy. After the war of liberation, the government decided to build the language institute here on our land that we never did own, but promised us dormitory housing and caretaker jobs for all their children. Within a year after the five of us moved into our dormitory room, our father died."

He stopped here and watched the waitress take down his lean-to and place its materials next to the fire ring. Sitting back on her rock, she added one piece at a time to keep the fire burning slowly.

"I had just started first grade, and was learning to write my first words, *Long Live Mao Zedong,* a hundred times in my blue exercise book. I had even written it three times with a stick in the dirt-yard in front of our dormitory. On the day my father died, I took revenge and scraped dirt over these first five words in the yard. But Mao lived on, smoking until he died in his 80s, having lived twice as long as my father. A year later my older brother decided to drop out of high school and start making some money, because he didn't want to be poor like a teacher, forester or farmer, because he didn't want to see our mother going to work everyday wearing her same janitorial-blue blazer for the rest of her life."

The fire was down again, and the supply of sticks from the lean-to depleted. So the waitress walked over to his side, picked up his rifle, carefully ejecting the four cartridges from its chamber and magazine, placed it on the fire's remaining coals and said, "This should keep it going for the rest of the story. Please continue."

"A few years later the Red Guards entered my high school and took over everything. One day as I walked down a hidden path by the school building, I saw our former history teacher sweeping the dirt and fallen leaves with a broom. In embarrassment, I pretended not to recognize him and he didn't look up, but he turned away from me as I passed him. At that point, I decided I didn't want to spend the rest of my life as an observer no passion can touch. It was then that I decided to become a teacher, even if the pay isn't good, and to teach others what I know. It was then I learned that one could not love the peasants and make a movie about us because none of us would want to watch it and be moved by it.

"So now I find myself in this seminar with this foreign expert who doesn't seem to care at all about what we really need. He re-

minds me of the Christian missionaries who came with the foreign
economic exploitation of our country in our earlier era. At least
the nuns seemed to care about us, even though we were not their
main agenda. At least I know about the dangers of this foreign exchange. But look, the sun is at least shining today. We Chinese
have always smiled through our worst adversities — maybe what
we need now is a big laugh. But we need to do something about
these walls first. The interior space they create fosters servility, re-
sentment and hatred, like the space for the peoples in Santiago,
Lima, Johannesburg, and the West Bank. Yesterday I bumped into
our professor at the post office. Either he didn't want to see me, or
pretended not to, same colonial thing. Later when I saw him jog-
ging around the inside path of the wall, I understood: he was con-
tinuing to navigate and define a course from which we must become increasingly more absent. I believe this, if I believe in anything at all inside a true story."

After he finished telling this story faithfully word by word, he
felt all the anxiety leave his heart. The waitress gave him his fortune cookie which blossomed into a simple message, *You will go
home to your story in peace,* and disappeared. He continued sitting
by the warmth of the fire, and decided that he would not try to
second-guess what he could remember of his adopted west.

Digging From China

I tried and tried
To dream a place where nothing was the same
— Richard Wilbur

Ge thought quickly, a wrong decision now would mean the end of the people on Liuheng Dao, an island society whose existence depended entirely on its tea production, the *Camellia sinesis* var. *assamica* Kit introduced to develop an economy since the country's recent liberation. Reliance on the slow but natural seed propagating itself in such a small and cool area did not effectively compete with the larger mainland cooperative tea farms in the southern provinces where it was warmer. Ge was working on a different approach in his micro-laboratory, trying to beat nature with a quicker tissue-culture method. Right now he had to decide, as the thin shadow of a tea leaf slivered into his eye pressed to the electronic microscope, if risking another dissection would destroy the entire dream for years.

He decided to make another slice, and his fingers were ready for it, the lives of 2,831 people on the edge with him, manipulating the digital scalpel into place before starting the cut. It was beginning to work, a layer slowly peeling away, a duplicate copy unveiling underneath, its DNA hyphenated in its imaging. His breathing relaxed, the earlier trials worth the patience which he continued to exercise over this final cloning. In these last months he had sacrificed almost everything, the graduate students under his direction, his weekend visits with his only grandson, his music.

Ge carefully made the final separation, rechecked the humidity level in the storage vessels before inserting the identical halves, and placed them side by side in the same compartment in the locked refrigeration tank. After recording this data on his computer file and sending a copy to the Ministry of Experiment's terminal, he turned off everything, finally the lights.

When he got back to his apartment, he started opening the stack of mail that had accumulated since the beginning of his project. He opened a two-year old package from a friend in Boston, and found a trowel inside. The attached note said, *I tried to dig a hole straight down with this trowel from the shed, far enough for China, damn it, and sweating like a coolie, but ended up in the middle of the Indian Ocean instead. Where are you? Love, Annie.*

Ge looked at the trowel from Annie's shed and wondered if this was the same one Marco Polo had used to find China seven centuries ago. He decided to try digging the other way, damn it, and find out if he would sweat like a *Meiquo qui zi* and end up somewhere in the Americas. So he hefted the tool from hand to hand, and it felt just right — a little more or a little less would have meant certain disaster. He started the digging in his bedroom, beginning with the carpet, then the floor's plaster and wood, straight down past his sleeping neighbors, professors who had published too much of nothing, and into the ground for days and nights without food or resting, not even when he got closer to the center where the digging was much easier and things were beginning to change into their other halves, jettisoned hats, round trip tickets, insistent poems.

The compass around his neck that had kept him true on the way down, and his log tables and slide rule calculations fixed earth's exact center, directing him into a reversal. Even though his wrists and arms were not tired, Ge was surprised by the difficulty of digging up. As it became harder and harder the farther he got away from the center, he distracted himself by thinking about what language he would have to use after he surfaced, if he could get away with palindrome, a trick he had picked up drinking with Annie at the Ritz years ago when they were students, or if he will not be discovered for days in enemy country south of the Equator, and if life would not be the same after this.

He held his breath as the feel of Annie's trowel signaled that he was getting close to the top, only a few cubic meters left to dig, and soon there, tilting the blue of a different but widening sky, and life after all by the side of a street cafe in downtown Buenos Aires, a couple staring at the emerging Ge in astonishment, their drinks half finished in the deepening afternoon air.

While he finished dusting himself, the street swelled with curious onlookers. Soon the police arrived, then the Absent Minister with the key to the city, and after the appropriate welcoming speeches, Ge was escorted in Spanish to a hotel where a shower and fresh change of clothes made him feel he was on the edge of a divided dream in which no half was the same and each was something new, something different. Dressing in front of the mirror, he caught a glimpse of his other self looking out all day and finding all the tea in China under his other orderly eye.

Definitions

Shun Min was assigned the news anchoring position right after graduation from the national broadcasting institute. At three hours a day, ten days a month, no writing or editing or reporting stories, just show up in time for makeup before noon and before six to read the news, it was easy enough, the envy of his classmates who were given jobs as video librarian, station timekeeper and boom operator. For the first two years he put all of himself into his work, each story he read, however short and sometimes ambiguous, carried his most sincere and believable expressions, his voice pulsing with heart-felt humanity, assuring his viewers of the safe passage of another day. *Trust me, trust me* he had said at least five hundred times a year in the privacy of four million homes, *I will not lie to you,* and the people in the capital believed him, even when the lights sometimes reflected off his glasses. On the streets he was easy to recognize, and citizens would stop him and articulate their trust, sometimes touching a hand or sleeve, and once, in this country where things numinous have been banned since its liberation in 1949, an elderly woman limping on her left side lightly tugged one of his ears just to make sure he was not divinity itself.

This April when he was reading a brief story on the evening news about the student gathering at Tiananmen Square, a wisp of anxiety appeared in his eyes, and for the remaining minutes before the camera focused on the international weather map, his voice sounded distracted, then stumbled once on the temperatures between Karachi and Cairo. After the broadcast, the news producer approached him, concerned about his health and diet. The station manager offered a car to take him home. Slightly cautious from all this attention, he said *I'm all right* carefully three times before they believed him, then rode his bicycle home after wiping off his makeup going down in the elevator. In the approaching twilight of another promising spring sunset, Shun wondered about riding downtown to see the students, but not being a reporter, he went home instead, mentally counting the number of times these students have gathered here in Beijing: 1900, 1911, 1927, 1966, 1976, and now in 1989, seven times this century, although he was not sure 1966 should be included.

That evening as he continued reading another novelist preoccupied with the scar on the national conscience left there by the three years of political aberration between 1966 and 1969 — a wound so deep that even now a generation later people still refuse to talk about it, as if it had completely vanished, or had not happened at all, which Shun knew was not true — he heard a loud knocking on his apartment door. All evening he had heard the repeated sirens of police and emergency vehicles passing in the streets, and the excited voices of his neighbors who had gone to investigate the rumors, but as a news professional, he knew that such compulsive curiosity could wait until the stories came into the studio in the morning, after they had been gathered, sorted and checked by knowledgeable persons trained and experienced in interpreting these dramatic events. All he would have to do was read them, all there in the past perfect tense.

A tall man in a long coat introduced himself politely, though he did not need to since Shun recognized him as a key member of the central party's policy-making bureau. Over his shoulders, Shun could see the shapes of two other men standing in the background, away from the light.

I can only stay a minute, the bureau member said, let's not waste it standing on ceremony. From your broadcast tonight, we were worried about you. He paused, letting his message enough time to sink in. Then he asked, Have you been wondering what's happened to the students?

No, I don't think so, Shun answered.

Do you think like your neighbors that some students have disappeared? That the PLA are responsible?

No, I didn't know my neighbors thought that. I didn't even know there were any soldiers.

Those are only irresponsible rumors uttered by peasants. You have done a famous job on television, and we want to encourage and help you, and then with both hands he flashed open his long coat.

Its folds were lined with sheets and sheets of stamped official papers. Here, he said, removing a set from the left and handing it to Shun, here, he said, this will help you understand our deliberated position. This is your new definitive dogma on disappearance. But there's no need to read it, it's official, he added. It says that information transmitters are forbidden to convey stories about disappearances, ever. They're demoralizing; they can panic the people and destabilize the government. Besides, it's not true: it's not scientific, people don't just disappear.

They both stood there a moment thinking about what had just been said. Shun could hear a man outside his apartment thumbing a butane cigarette lighter, *click, click, click,* before it was lost in the sound of another passing siren, before that too was replaced by a soft but distinct knocking on his door.

I must go now, the bureau member said and shook Shun's hand.

After he left, Shun continued standing in the middle of his apartment until the official papers dropped forgetfully from his hand. He then spent the rest of the night in a living room chair thinking about what the bureau member had said. Was his visit a warning? It definitely was not a routine visit announcing a policy change — that would surely have gone to the station manager or news director. And why me, he thought, I just read the news that's handed to me ten minutes before I go on the air. Did I betray something when I read the student story tonight? And soldiers? And disappearances? How does one read a story about disappearances, after all? What would be its effect? And who would believe it? Who can authenticate it he asked himself, until he remembered some stories he had read in a grey-market American newsmagazine one day when he was waiting for someone in a downtown joint venture hotel lobby, some stories about people disappearing in green Ford Falcons in Argentina and others losing themselves in Los Alamos just before Japan surrendered in 1945. But maybe these were not the same things. Maybe, maybe, he repeated to himself until it was beginning to get light outside.

The news director wasn't in his office when Shun went to see him the next morning. All of the drawers of the news archivist's filing cases and desks were opened however, overflowing with papers, more as if someone had been trying to file them away than remove them. Shun picked up a sheet of paper from the many that were scattered on the floor. *Dateline Buenos Aires, August 7, 1977. Disappeared today, Pepe, Marianna and Angela Mendoza, father, wife and daughter, 27, 24 and infant, witnesses said, whisked away in a green Ford Falcon while they were walking along Avenida Florida in broad daylight. No known political activism or membership.* Shun picked up another one, a similar disappearance, Shanghai 1937, then Selma 1966, Warsaw 1945, and on and on, the room full of it, until he got to Hiroshima and Nagasaki 1945.

Dazed, he walked into the lobby and did not see anyone there at all, only gaps where they should have been. As he started out the sliding glass doors of the station building, he noticed too that everything on the outside had entirely disappeared, all of Beijing had absolutely vanished, everything except for his exact double, another Shun Min, walking up the sidewalk to the building as if it too had disappeared. He knew this to be true, he said to himself, because he could tell this story now in the first person, a choice he did not have yesterday.

Smoke

for Joy

Shen Zang was walking to his office when he was picked up by two agents and rushed across town in an unmarked car. Police and fire trucks surrounded the Bank of China building when they arrived, everyone looking up at the woman hanging by her fingers on the ledge of the thirteenth floor.

How long has she been there, Shen asked.

We don't know for sure. Some have said two hours, others, all her life, and that person over there, the captain said, shaking his walkie-talkie's rubber antenna in the direction of a Creek woman with a saxophone case, she said five hundred years.

These answers have become more ambiguous since Shen became the first head of the recently established Ministry of Therapy. Within two days after his appointment appeared in the official newspaper, strangers would stop him in the streets with their detailed life stories, some offering reasons to live, others he wasn't so sure. As the director of this national repository of mental health in a modernizing nation, he had to accept these offers of advice, even when he could not distinguish rumor from lore, or report from minimalism. Last week he had to confront a case of a man who threatened to drown himself in two inches of basin water, and mediate between the Premier and his wife who was threatening to leave him for Henry Kissinger. In fact, he has yet to reappear in his office since the first two days of his appointment, and he has yet to learn the size, function and names of his staff, and the linkages with other ministries and emergency units.

Do you have a net? Shen asked the police captain.

A net? Why? If she wants to jump, she jumps.

But my job is to stop her.

That's not mine. I'm here for crowd control, and to investigate how someone could have passed through a Bank of China security window. Maybe the fire captain has a net.

Shen could sense that the onlookers were beginning to get anxious, that something tragic was about to happen. From his United States psychiatric training that specialized in coincidental meanings, he had learned to tell when everything will arrive perfectly in time, and when it won't. This was a won't, unless something intervened quickly.

The fire captain had already radioed for a net, but at this moment he was busily coordinating a surgical extraction operation between his rappelling crew waiting on the fifteenth floor, and the police's anti-student-terrorist squad on the eleventh. So Shen took the express elevator up to the thirteenth, and cautiously approached the opened window.

Don't come any closer, she said.

Shen assured her that he wouldn't, that he just wanted to talk with her, that he had a story which she must listen to if she has hung on to life for so long.

Don't you want to hear why I'm here trying to end my life?

Yes, of course, but will you come back up if I listened?

There was no answer, and in her silence Shen began to describe the group of one hundred women dressed in black who have gathered everyday for three years in Jerusalem, a silent protest against oppression. Every day rightists and leftists by jeeploads encircle them, spitting at them, but they say nothing, and return again the next day. They have done this before, most recently in Buenos Aires and Greenham Common, these mothers who look after our promises.

Ask yourself this, Shen said at the end, ask yourself what kind of promises they have made to each other.

There was a slight sigh, as if the wind had carried it up from the Creek woman with the saxophone case. Then she added, if I do, will you trade places with me?

Shen looked down at the uplifted faces thirteen floors below, the fire trucks and police vans, and then at the woman's fingers clinging to the ledge, a perfect heartbeat in the middle of the current.

Morning Stars

Count them each, bright and clear, there are enough for everyone. There is no need to ask if there are enough, unless you are Li Hsi-fan and arranging to hold up the Bank of China's headquarters on Beijing's busy Fuchengmen in order to finance another revolution. Now Li is not just nobody, having spent a good part of his adult life every October 1 standing to Mao's left in the reviewing stands in Tiananmen Square, a privileged position he had earned after saving *A Dream of Red Mansions* from Beida's bigwig literary autobiographers' death blow. Now at fifty-five and recently retired as an editor for *The People's Daily*, Li has been trying to redirect his life into another just cause, especially after he learned that the most popular American novels in China since its liberation in 1949 were Mark Twain's *The Adventures of Tom Sawyer*, followed closely by Margaret Mitchell's *Gone with the Wind*. The first he doesn't feel so badly about, although he is somewhat ambiguous about the model Tom might provide Chinese middle schoolers, but the second, well, the second he thought is worth about a 20-fen postage stamp, not enough to send a letter out of the country.

So each day as he plots the details for the heist on his early morning walks, he counts the stars, his morning stars, each minute twinkle contributing another contingency: definitely masks and guns (how else can he force the issue?), even though the bank has no guards (there has been no bank robbery reported in China since 1949, not even in Shanghai or Guangzhou — as a journalist for thirty-five years with daily access to China's only news source, the *Xinhua,* he knows this to be true — thefts, graft, corruption and embezzlement, yes, but bank robbery? definitely not): only foreign currencies in big denominations; hitting the bank at one in the afternoon so that they can make a quick getaway by its closing hour at four; a crew of sixty-two, thirty-one for each of the main floors where the cash and certificates are kept; using bicycles instead of vans so that they can disappear more easily into the rush-hour gridlock of five million other bicyclists; and six superfast counters, since the cashiers most certainly won't let them out of the bank until the money has been counted at least three times by three different persons.

These superfast counters would be easy to locate. Li had just seen a group of third graders on national television who could count trillions faster than any calculator or abacus. They could be trusted for this project, considering they have probably seen the movie version of Tom Sawyer. But what about the remaining fifty-five? Li personally knew hundreds who have been vilified with sufficient motivation for revenge, but he was not sure which ones could be trusted and which ones would be travelling betrayers looking for a quick exoneration. Perhaps having been separated from their parents during the years of political aberration could be a reliable criterion, thus putting them in their late thirties or early forties. Perhaps women who have found out that the people's liberation did not include them would be another good one, and that would mean all women over thirty. Definitely not anyone in their twenties, those children born since the cultural revolution to parents who had spoiled them in compensation for their own lost childhoods. And definitely not relatives. But fifty-five? How could Li find fifty-five who could be trusted, one of whom would have to double as a babysitter for the grade schoolers? Jesus of Nazareth could not find even twelve, and that was for all the marbles.

This is the day now, after months of locating the fifty-five adults Li thought he could trust, at least until the end of the day. They arrive singly or in pairs, and park their bicycles near the bank. The six look-alike grade schoolers are herded by their sitter, a woman in her late thirties, and together they resemble a group of school children about to tour the bank with their teacher, not an unusual occurrence here. Their plan is to enter the bank in small numbers, meet on the long stairway between the first and second floors where they will put on their silk stockinged masks and take out their Uzis from the suitcases, a popular item used to carry large quantities of money into the bank, which they will use to carry out the notes at four.

The electric eye to the automatic sliding glass doors is not working. The doors do not open! As his comrades gather about him, Li could see through the tinted glass that work inside the bank has come to a standstill. Every cashier and teller on the first floor has gathered behind the janitor trying to manually open the doors with a makeshift ratchet. The area managers are giving directions, but it does not help.

Li is getting frustrated, but used to waiting for everything from the very conventional to the inexplicable, the rest of them wait outside patiently and inconspicuously in the gathering throng. A friend says to him, "This confusion will help us," and another, "This will make it easier." So they wait. But after thirty minutes, Li begins to get agitated. One of the grade schoolers has to go to the bathroom, and his teacher takes him around the corner and comes back too much later, her fingers indicating Number Two to Li.

After another thirty minutes, Li elbows his way to the doorway and begins shouting, "I want your money; let me in, I want your money."

Someone inside says something, but Li cannot hear it. The janitor is beginning to invent another lever with letter openers and paper clips to turn the doors manually.

"What?" Li shouts.

An area manager inside uses his bullhorn this time.

"You have to wait until the doors are open."

"But I need it now."

The manager again, "Why are you in such a hurry? Everybody's in a hurry. Last week we had a woman who wanted to jump from the thirteenth floor window, this week you want your money now when you are still outside. You must wait — we are not open for business."

All the tellers and cashiers are now pressing their faces against the glass windows and doors to see what is happening outside. First their noses get squashed and distorted and turn into hog snouts, then their cheeks into perfect pancakes the size of paper-moon cutouts used to decorate the autumn festival. The janitor has abandoned his task and added his flattened prints to the glass also. The grade schoolers are laughing hysterically, as well as their teacher-sitter.

Li continues to yell "I want your money now."

A few of his accomplices are beginning to leave, shaking their heads. The area manager continues to yell at Li with the bullhorn that he has to wait to get the money until he gets in, after the door is fixed. Another grade schooler has to go, and this time the teacher takes the whole group and never returns. More of the adults leave, including the only relative Li thought he could trust enough to include in the heist. The crowd is thinning out too, even the foreign-looking lady with the music case who looks as if her ancestors could have been Chinese of ten thousand years past. Even the tellers and the cashiers on the inside are getting bored by the endless repetition.

Finally there is only Li left on the outside and the janitor on the inside. Li approaches the glass door, drops his suitcase, and puts his face and hand prints on the glass door right in front of the janitor who has jumped back. Then Li turns around and walks away, silently counting the amount of money he imagines he has taken from the bank. When he gets on his bicycle, he wonders if he has enough to take him to a South American country to buy up all the green Ford Falcons used by the secret police, and if this attempted robbery will not be reported by *Xinhua*. Even now with the wind at his back, Li wonders if it ever happened at all, which he knows is not enough for the twenty-first century.

The Connoisseur Of Chaos

And of ourselves and of our origins
ghostlier demarcations, keener sounds.
— Wallace Stevens

Mao Zedong had been in this library before, maybe seventy-one years ago exactly, here, looking at the same history books that he was to have shelved yesterday, not reading them but knowing what they promise for his imagination, looking out the dusty window to the sun setting on farmers seeding in the fields in another March or this March or not March at all, but April or May in 1918. That same night or another night, he may well have dreamed that soldiers were beating down his door as his friends gathered theory and strategy in secrecy, but woke up before they had a chance to bust through to a darkened room and see him sitting upright in bed and sweating and reaching for a cigarette like his namesake, but at least knowing from the shape of his cassette player against the window that this is now his room in 1989, and it is March, the planning meeting safely over, and the blood-soaked fields he saw from the library window zoned out in the last forty years of Beijing's annexation. Be cautious of involving the workers in your arrangements, someone had warned, it can easily end up in chaos, or worse.

After holding out for several weeks against an equally stubborn central committee, the students were beginning to get impatient and anxious. Mao was the first to get off the Boeing 747 in San Francisco, where a crowd of mainlander well-wishers, friends of the movement and reporters had gathered to greet him. He tucked in his shirt and gave a speech. Tiananmen Square was almost completely jammed with people, but somehow food had managed to get in and people out to the airport safely, the traffic-controlling students magically opening instant lanes for the occasional ambulance needed by an aspiring dissident.

Mao's girlfriend tugged at his sleeves while he was being interviewed on CNN. He must get out, disperse the crowd now, there will be trouble. At breakfast on June 3, her well-placed father had instructed her not to go to the square anymore, that she and her Uygar boyfriend must stay away. The urgency in his voice convinced her, but Mao would not listen to her, that short irreversible step between imagination and memory. As the coordinator of the information center he could not leave, he had to stay to wrangle with rumors, examine the sources of misinformation, and disseminate the occasional news releases to the salivating international press gathered here for Gorbachev's visit. After he gave another speech into a VOA microphone, a girl yelled into the gathering twilight, "Mao Zedong! I love you!" and he replied, "Me too, I love myself too!", somewhere between his personal act of survival and uncontrollable public weeping. At the main terminal a FAX message waited for him: *Congratulations on your Nieman scholarship at Harvard. Count on me for support. Best regards, Edward Kennedy.* Already in the visible distance the PLA was gathering in numbers, but the students were convinced that this was not Hungary, that this was an army of the people's liberation, that the soldiers were on their side. Somewhere in there Mao attended a few classes, but it must have been in Cambridge a few weeks later because one morning a prompted message appeared on his computer screen: YOU ARE DRINKING THE BLOOD OF THE STUDENTS.

Some students from an engineering university were operating a portable generator to help Mao's lap-top computer keep track of the accumulating information that was beginning to arrive faster than the Kentucky Fried Chicken donated by interested downtown merchants. Sometime in here he found a Chinese restaurant in Boston, and after ducking a 7.62 bullet between the lions at Tiananmen Square more than half a century ago, he almost took it again from a Chinese waiter's meat cleaver for not leaving a tip in his attempt to break from his country's past, its corruption, nepotism, the hopelessness of opium, the right indistinguishable from the left, the absence of dreams. Events were accelerating beyond the organizers' anticipation, and with the whole world watching, it was becoming almost impossible now to distinguish between rumor and lore, just as it was for countless previous generations. Next it was lunch with Marlon Brando at Taos and later dinner with Andrei Sakharov in Boston before establishing a computer information network for the movement at Brandeis.

At the moment when he was paying the least attention after several sleepless days and nights, Mao was astonished by the keener sound of fire-crackers popping off to the west of the square on Fuxingmen where the workers had gathered in great numbers, but he was not surprised, until he recognized it as the dull stutter of automatic gunfire. Mao's computer hit the concrete under the tent, and amidst the screaming and stench of smoke and popping of exploding bodies, several questions floated into the air: ABORT? IGNORE? RETRY? ESCAPE? For a moment he thought about changing his life now and removing his name from history, in the name of the father.

The Hyphen

He came here from someplace far away, Santiago, Johannesburg or more likely Lhasa, judging from his color. It is a very common occurrence now, these solitary daily arrivals. Most of their stories are the same, hunger and the lack of hope making their choice of leaving their home of 2,000 years a terribly simple thing.

Most of the time Ge didn't hear his mother's cry, but every night he could feel it in his sleep, separated from her by blankets of bloated children in a mud hut full of empty bowls. Then one morning three months ago he saw her by the washbasin looking at the sliver of a mirror stuck to the wall before she stepped back, knocked over the basin, and screamed for all of them.

There was a clarity in her scream, and it transformed itself into Ge's resolve to leave for the capital where he had heard reports of opportunity. So he slipped away one night and made his way slowly, selling some of the hard, black bread he had saved and doing odd jobs along the way. Only once did he regret not having said a word to his family, but he knew his sister would understand. He had planned to send them money, and to send for his brothers.

The doors were not as welcome as Ge had anticipated. It was difficult for him to move past the initial itinerancy of such short work as mucking, sweeping and carrying heavy loads on his shoulders, scrounging from throwaways to fill his metal *fanhe,* and catching naps in some abandoned doorway. But one morning he got lucky and met an elderly man out exercising his birds by slowly swinging their cage as he walked. Impressed by his questions, the man explained that his canaries understood that it was just an illusion, that this was just a difference held together by a linguistic hinge, and that like his birds, he's not in a position to change it. In the end the man took Ge to a construction site and introduced him to a foreman, a relative. Since Ge could hold a straight line, he worked with bricks, mostly resurfacing curbs and low retaining walls by himself. The work was dirty, monotonous, the tools always breaking, and the pay wasn't good. There was nothing left after meager meals and shared shelter. Ge wanted more. He wanted to acquire a skill that would qualify him for a resident red card and party membership, anything that would acknowledge his existence.

One evening as he walked by the window of a restaurant on his way to a public washing faucet, he saw a couple at a table near the window eating a dish that he recognized from pictures as having made this city famous. Eager to have a closer look, and perhaps even a taste of this roast duck, he gathered himself, brushed his hair back and entered. The couple at the table was outraged at being publicly assaulted like this by this ethnic tribesman, and immediately insisted the management detain Ge while they telephoned for a public security agent.

As soon as the agent arrived, Ge was whisked out of the restaurant and into the waiting unmarked vehicle, headed for the interrogation center. But Ge never made it there. How do I know this? I was the agent who picked him up, but after he told me his wretched story on the way downtown, I decided to change his destiny and dropped him off at the edge of his life, muttering something about having to learn to bridge the difference between survival and hope. Next day at the construction site no one even knew that he wasn't there anymore. But I must remain anonymous about this, if I don't want my own destiny changed. I don't know, but lately I've been beginning to feel that I haven't been here either — I don't know how else to tell this.

Reductions

From where Ge was looking up at the mountains in front of him with the filled water-pack on his back, the entire forest appeared to be on fire. Fresh firefighters were lined up and ready every twenty meters, their new yellow plastic hardhats edging the blackened ground as far as he could see to his sides, anxiously waiting for their leader's whistle signal to begin in unison. He recognized some of them as his students who had come up with him on the train from Beijing, in response to the Forestry Ministry's call for volunteers to suppress a fire two months out-of-control.

He exploits this story now two winters later as he can no longer tell for sure how old he is. Ever since the directive came down from the bureau last month deducting ten years from everyone's age, Ge has been confused about his life and what he wanted to do with it. At first he welcomed the official edict, and saw it as an inspired healing of the national wound, giving back to the people the ten years they had lost to the cultural revolution, but now he isn't so sure. By now everyone's birth certificate, residence booklet, work permit and identity card have been meticulously changed, not only erasing a decade of aberration, but also reflecting a gift of youth from the government, along with the forty kilos of cabbage which every domiciled citizen receives at the end of every harvesting season.

At twenty-one then, Ge is teaching graduate students who are thirteen years old, and of late they are begging to act that age too, screaming *Yi-Er-San-Si* as they skip rope, practice the latest disco steps or play badminton in the hallways between classes. Some of them were with him on the Black Dragon fire in the Hinggan Forest two years ago when the signal was given to press the starter button for the tiny Canadian motor on their pack to begin pumping the piddly ten liters of water onto the raging forest fire. He doubts that they can remember this now, nor would they want to. In this cold month of January in Beijing, such loss is easier to see, along with the shared cabbage wasting in every quadrangle of every *hutong*.

The student in Ge's office is beginning to get nervous, alternately twisting one clenched hand inside the palm of her other. After acing the TOEFL test, she had asked Ge for advice on her application letter for admission to the medical school at Columbia. Ge is challenging her inclusion of her hobbies — stamp collecting, listening to American country music, badminton — in her letter as coy and ridiculous. She purses her lips and begins to contrive the ritual sulk, but before she can convince herself of it, Ge asks her how she can worry about such trivia when only a few short months ago more than two hundred people were shot at Tiananmen Square, the same number that burned to death at the Da Xinan fire because the ministry did not have the foresight to evacuate them. Ge does not press the issue however, suspecting that the ministry had committed its economic vision to validating its newly invented backpacked water pumps instead of a fire detection and warning system. He also knows such details do not make any difference, since the student will not change anything in her letter anyway, that in asking him for advice she had merely followed a formality which was not of her own design either.

Alone in his office now, Ge wonders if he should take advantage of his new age and pursue another course of study that would lead to some other profession than teaching, maybe night courses in petroleum chemistry, where he might meet someone he would like to marry. Then would she be in her twenties, or teens, he asks himself; would she wear a big pink bow in her hair, or would she have short hair; would he introduce her to his parents as a girl or a woman? He is coming closer and closer to the conclusion that the age deduction directive was a mistake, that experiences in life, however tragic and painful, cannot be erased by some administrative decree, however studied.

Furthermore, if ten years are to be deducted from his age, exactly which ten years have been erased? If Ge is now twenty-one, does it mean that he's lost the last ten years, including the memory of the fire and yesterday too; or the decade of upheaval between 1966 and 1976, as the government had intended in its lengthy deliberations, when he was in grade school and middle-school? Despite the heroic efforts of man and technology, the fire at Da Xinan burned itself out when the rainy fall weather set in, just as it had started, when several lightning burns merged and defined their own course. Now the ministry is again asking for volunteers, this time to re-seed the burned-out hundreds of thousands of hectares in the spring, as if nature cannot heal itself.

Although Ge doesn't feel like going home, he buttons up his coat, puts on his gloves and waits until he is warm enough before mounting his bicycle. Is this all there is in life, futilely arguing with a student over what she should include in her medical school

application letter, mentally bashing the Forestry Ministry for playing around with its miniscule water pumps while the whole forest
burned up, and now wondering which years of his life have been
redeemed? Urging his toes down on the pedals, Ge imagines that
in spite of everything, he will live on forever in the dust of stones,
his memory ever shifting, no matter what is said or written, to save
us our worries, our troubles, and yes, even our sighs.

Keepers

Xiao Baba slowly riffled through the thick sheets of the picture album a second time, craning his neck over the colored images for a closer look. Each photograph shifted a little, but enough to blur his most rudimentary visual distinctions in life — eyeglasses became mountain peaks; a ship's prow merged with the tail plumage of a Quetzal; his father into his son; his son-father, himself; man, woman — and as his eyes got used to this way of looking at life, everything became everything else against an expanding universe of colors.

He left the album open on an 8 x 10 enlargement of a high mountain lake, took his shoes and socks off and tucked them safely out of the way under his desk. The ducks and the dogs were already in the water when Xiao Baba slipped himself into the lake for the long swim across the deep-edged immensity. After his strokes and breathing became effortless and regular and he knew it was then possible, he began to exist, and he knew it. He wanted to believe that the birds and plants had left their pre-Darwinian taxonomic and specimen graveyards, that the animals had ceased being victims of tireless human cruelty and were gathered now in such constant murmur. But Xiao Baba knew better — this could not be true, realism cannot be usurped, history is history. So he focused his attention instead on the topographical legends of the approaching opposite shore, its beach shimmering in the glare of the noonday sun.

Leaving the short drop of beach behind him, Xiao Baba walked onto the parapets of a citrus county, its fruit furiously clapping with immense answers. On the next terrace in front of a shelter, the caretaker couple, runaways from the Guatemalan highlands, was answering some questions of travel asked by another, more recent defector, a Tiananmen Square mainlander. Together they accepted some food and something to drink offered in any language, shaded in the hint of a banyan tree from Xiao Baba's distant childhood, lingering, marveling at the spread of sky, at the shifting wind in their lives, and at the color of the dissenting nationalist.

From this origin of hyphens, they weaved their stories unhurriedly, an occasional aaa-eh acknowledging their intricate extensions, because they knew they were true even if it had not happened to them, even if it had no endings. Now and then a few ducks drifted in between their elaborations and settled at the crumbs by their side, their feet free of market ties. By then a light wind had carried the thousand paper cranes from Hiroshima, and what it brought reminded them to renew their determination.

Xiao Baba stood up to leave, but as he took a last look at the Guatemalan couple and the Beijing student, he knew he was them, there by the side of the shelter, and they were him, in this orchard, here now swimming strong, back across the lake there in that color photograph here together with the ducks and the dogs, in this picture that is every picture ever, that he no longer needed because this will become the memory that would keep and not shift and change, that this will be hope looking for a random child to give itself to, like that one waiting at the West Bank, rock already in hand, wishing that he understood more about the dust of stones and the shifting strata beneath the ground on which he stood in his socks and his shoes.

Disturbances

I was always careful when I went to sleep at night, sometimes waiting for the rain to come first, and then asking for its permission. In these winters then, sleep is always brittle, little dream slivers waiting to be disturbed. What I have lost is the ability to sleep, here in the northern solstice, where darkness never seems to disappear entirely, always its shadow remaining, lingering just beyond my perception of distance, always shifting, waiting.

That is another thing I say when I write from this country, not knowing if these letters will ever get home. To increase their chances of getting past the censors, I keep them bland and non-controversial. I first send formal greetings, and inquire about the family members, carefully using the right number. Then I talk about the weather, and up here where I've been assigned for the duration, that's easy. I just repeat the exact same things that we talk about among ourselves every moment of every day — how cold it is in both Fahrenheit and Celsius, when it will snow next, what kind of snow, for how long, will there be wind with it, and how many weeks before it'll begin to thaw. Occasionally such a conversation at the canteen would seem a little too urgent, as if we were using the weather as a political barometer.

Not knowing who might be listening, or who might be the zealous cadre among us, we never talk about it directly, and go about our biological research as if there were no political aberration taking place in our mainland, as if there were no teenaged civilian guards marching through our neighborhoods every day and every night looking for evidence, however contrived, however circumstantial. As a resource biologist, I find it exceptionally difficult to ignore this, and too that our findings here are being used for military purposes.

Last September when the daylight started diminishing, Ge, our senior biologist in charge of the project, stammered something at breakfast about Yucatan, and banged his fist down on the table for emphasis. We had admired his capacity for moving over the tundra, his balance, and his occasional suggestions to help us accommodate ourselves to the diminutive biology in such expanses of geography and meteorology. So this morning we were all surprised by the violence in his voice, up here where everything is slightly reduced.

"We are where we go," Ge said, and added, "by moving, we make everything else move."

The rest of us looked around the table and, embarrassed and baffled, said nothing and stared down into our mugs.

"Yucatan," Ge said, rising, "Yucatan," again, as he slipped on his pack and left us sitting in the canteen.

That was the last any of us was to see him. When he didn't return by dinner, we got out our powerpacks and snowmobiles and started looking for him through the night, meticulously following sanctioned search-and-rescue procedures. After losing his tracks within two klicks of the station by daylight, we sent for the dogs, and then the cook, who has some native blood in him, but all to no avail.

When the weather started looking threatening on the second morning, we radioed in Ge's disappearance. That afternoon the commander of the region arrived with the superintendent of lost persons and a team of native trackers in two helicopters, and for the next three days, every effort at the station was directed at locating Ge.

One of the trackers found Ge's pack still sealed, its survival rations, flare pistol, and emergency bivouac shelter untouched. There was no sign that he had ever been there, except for the pack itself — Ge had simply vanished. Although we were used to persons vanishing every day and every night in the mainland, up here it was different, up here where nothing ever vanishes. So Ge's disappearance left a gap in the landscape, in our images of our lives.

For a month I could not write home — sending off a letter about the changing weather would have been contrived, and writing about his disappearance would have certainly invited serious consequences, the letter certain never to get beyond the volunteer mail censors. At the station we went about our work averting each other's glances, even at the canteen, as if we were all waiting for someone else to say something first, listening ever so sensitively for the slightest seismic disturbance to openly suggest that we were all thinking about the exact same thing.

But nothing like that happened, and by now, four months later, Ge has probably become for us someone almost entirely symbolic, I'm afraid, someone even he would hardly recognize. Perhaps it will always be a little like this, this perception of waiting, shifting, this darkness lingering, until this distance too is forgotten and becomes equal. Until then, I am always very careful about sleeping in it.

Old Hearts

As long as there shall be stones,
the seeds of fire will not die.

— Lu Xun

This is a house, and it does not have a door. In its place, choose an empty space, whether square, rectangle or circle, or any shape of your imagining, and walk through it with scruples. Our history is a history of doors and passages, of light to dark, or dark to light, or those journeys in between. But there is no door to this house, and we have already passed through it.

In the light a student has picked up a rock. He hefts its weight in his hand and, taking careful aim at a tank the color of dirt, he heaves it. It strikes the turret mount with a hollow metallic sound and bounces back into the street. Cameras from near and far record this moment. One of their pictures will later be used to arrest him. Is this why we have walked through the space of the house without a door, to see this and record it too? That student might well disappear later, depending on how far we've come, and give us an ending, a void in our hearts signifying his time and his place forever; and if we've come far enough, or not nearly far enough, his mothers would then collect his promises and gather in front of the ministry in silent vigil.

But we are too far off ourselves, as reliable as the metaphors seem to be. So let's step aside and check our omissions and exaggerations. There, the sun is rising unstoppable, nothing turning it back there. There are walls here too, some covered with revolutionary words, *THE BIRD STILL LIVES* in several colors. The only sound rising from the thronging crowd is an inept gasp anticipating irreversible dreams. We must move cautiously here, renew our identities, cross our hearts, if we are to avoid the stray lunatic endangering every species.

Then, there is that ten year old girl whose parents have left her to the side of her life, or she has left them, there's no escaping it, it's all the same in this kind of accident. She is taking a pause here too, standing before Bogota or Shanghai, while across the street history is defining its own martial laws. With some spaces still empty in our passports, there is no reason why we can't take her with us. She shrugs and says *Will there be the sound of shooting where we go?* The dreams are thickest here where there is no room for error. Even the promises that have stayed around long enough not to be noticed are beginning to fluctuate. They are saying *Look here, Look here* in as many possible voices waiting to be counted. There are no explanations, and most of the time we don't even hear them, not even their symptoms, being what they are.

Look, the sky is beginning to close, we must go before the curfew descends on us. Remember, the house we return to is the same one without the door. By now we must know exactly which one it is because we have never seen it before. Come, you too, we do not lie, not even secretly.

Cadenzas

I take the melodic line and push it
past history and imagination —
then I pelt it with eggs until it comes
back, quick and unrelenting.

— Beethoven, on the 18 cadenzas he
wrote for Mozart's piano concertos

W hen there was enough to fill all the ballots in the room,
Arias embraced the particulars and stood up. Believe me, it
all happened so very fast that no one knew for sure it wasn't an act
of the imagination. Count them, he said, count them to be sure
this isn't something we'd find in tomorrow's papers. It was just as
he had said, each piece of paper unfolding all our signed promises
of secrecy. There was no dissension.

In a special edition the next morning, the opposition printed
the story anyway, and it included specific names, dates and places
for the most part as truthfully as we had gathered. Arias called just
before the story came on the radio and television. We have been
betrayed, we all promised to be silent, but someone has betrayed
us, he said. I tried to tell him it'll be all right, that there was no
proof, no corroborating pictures to make them credible, that the
republic will not panic. But Arias reminded me we didn't have any
picture either — yet we believed these disappearances have occurred like before, much as we often place our trust in random

93

coincidences and wild repetitions and in fact have come to expect them like children — and then disappeared entirely, his voice trailing into thin air.

By the time of the emergency council meeting that afternoon, only four of us showed up. We sat at one end of the long conference table trying to reconstruct the details one by one, repeating them again and again, trying to be sure we had not left out anything, anything at all.

Section III

Section III

The Catholic All-Star Chess Team

It is the queen which gives the king most
trouble in this game and all the other
pieces support her.

— Teresa of Avila

My most immediate reason for recording this story is my suspicion that the monogamous obsession of the Chinese for the game of bridge will prompt them, when the island reverts to Chinese sovereignty in 1997, to dismiss from history a most incredible chess match that occurred in the middle of the century in the present British crown colony of Hong Kong. I myself do not play bridge, ever since I once read Arthur Schnabel refer to the game as a disease contracted by the demented. In fact, his warning was so severe that I have never even had a friend who played bridge. I do not pretend to understand the game, but I know enough about bridge and the Chinese to know that, like everyone else, they will most likely rewrite Hong Kong's cultural history and relegate chess to a game played by students at the King George V School during the colonial period.

As a matter of fact I did not attend KGV, but in the early 1950s played on the chess team for my required intramural activity at the Diocesan Boys School when Governor Grantham, a wood-pusher known for his quirky gambling habits, formed a formidable team with seven of the finest local players, including one International

Master, an official with the Hang Seng Bank who also sat on the Legislative Council, with His Excellency playing in the last position to round out the eight, and invited local teams to a two-week June Tournament for the Governor's Challenge Cup and a HK$4,000 cash award.

The captains of the DBS and DGS teams got their players together one Saturday afternoon at my parents' apartment near the Royal Observatory to discuss fielding a joint team. The mood was at first pessimistic, since it seemed to most of us that such a junior tag team would be eliminated in the first round. But when Natalie Rodney, the captain of the DGS team who looked quite striking aggressively dressed in something other than her school blues and red tie, mentioned that we should do it if only to gain the competitive experience of playing under FIDE international competition rules, we became excited and were willing to enter the contest and be publicly humiliated by being seeded lowest in the field.

As we sipped our second shandygaffs, we started putting together the starting eight in that living room, surrounded by light tapestries and several orchids whose bent colored the striped greens of an early Hong Kong May. They came singing, deft trapezists certified in ubiquity and unanimity, whose names came to rest on the official entry form:

1. Teresa Avila
2. Ruy Lopez
3. Pia Lindstrom
4. Donald Chow
5. Vincent Lombardi
6. Peter Pluhta (capt.)

7. William Perry

8. Natalie Rodney

It would be most appropriate to chronicle the stories of such a historical assemblage in that international city:

1. TERESA AVILA : Her high school studies at DGS were cut short when her father was called back to Madrid. After a brief but trying early marriage to an itinerant poet, she turned to writing instructional books and moved to Carmel, California. Although Teresa gave up competitive chess quite early, she nevertheless used chess metaphors in her lessons, particularly her bestseller, *Way of Perfection,* which has since been translated into eighty-six languages at last count. She is perhaps even better known as the ecstatic model for the heir to the sewing machine dynasty, photographer Gianlorenzo Bernina.

2. RUY LOPEZ : After his graduation from DBS, he went professional and both became Grandmaster and approached a 2,600 points Elo-and Clarke Rating before his twenty-first birthday. The lure of big money attracted him, and for several years he made a handsome living decimating rich fish in blindfold simultaneous and odds games. According to his brother Barry who also graduated from DBS and now teaches writing at Notre Dame University in Indiana, Ruy soon tired of this decadent champagne-and - oysters-for-breakfast lifestyle and joined the priesthood the morning after his thirtieth birthday. The latest word from the alumni office tells that he is angling to make bishop.

3. PIA LINDSTROM: She took the Radcliffe team to a national collegiate team championship, and later an individual first in San Francisco in 1962 in the world's first televised chess match with a score of +4, =3, -1. Pia then joined NBC and is now one of its chief news executives.

4. DONALD CHOW : Undoubtedly the megabrain of the team, Don went to M.I.T. and changed the spelling of his last name to Zhou. He later programmed the MANIAC computer at Los Alamos and the IBM 704 at Livermore to play chess, and the MAC SHACK VI which provided Bobby Fischer an opponent for his last published games. It is rumored that on April 25, 1980, the day after the aborted Teheran extraction mission, he was appointed by the Pentagon to develop an interagency and interservice informational system with a Cray computer that allowed the SEALS and Delta counterterrorist units to instantly retrieve up-to-date human and signal intelligence.

5. VINCENT LOMBARDI : Always the optimist and the team's cheerleader, he urged us on with daily pre-match huddles and the rallying cry of *Go for daylight*, Vince toured Italy for a year after graduating from DBS before joining the meatpacking industry in Brown County, Wisconsin, giving up chess for bowling to keep himself trim.

6. PETER PLUHTA : Having survived the Warsaw Uprising as a six year old, Pete was a natural for the captain's position, since such survival instinct and temperament were essential to maintaining order and decorum among such a miscegenated team. At only slightly over six feet, he made it as a point guard on the Duquesne

University basketball team by virtue of his dunking skill. Sadly, he defected to the game of competitive bridge when he turned twenty-one, but has distinguished himself by playing on the team that has defeated the Dallas Aces on three consecutive 128-board matches for money.

7. WILLIAM PERRY : He had a solid but unimaginative game, never known for chancy or aggressive moves. Away from the board, however, he was accident prone, and often needed others to move his pieces for him when he surprised everyone by showing up at matches with both hands bandaged. It was conceded that he could not hurt us in playing the seventh position. After DBS he charged through Australia's restrictive immigration policies and went into the mobile refrigeration business.

8. NATALIE RODNEY : She was an enigma. We thought she was Russian. We knew that she lived near Causeway Bay, but that was all. Someone thought he saw her in Chicago's O'Hare Airport several years later, but he wasn't sure. I remember Natalie most for the image she projected that afternoon, and her name pencilled on the stone ledge of our apartment's veranda later, obviously put there by my sister to establish credibility for her allegation that I had a crush on her.

As it was that will never be again, we prepared for the challenge, tested each other on the variants of all the major modern openings, simulated each other's games, played blindfolded to increase concentration, anticipated the best and the worst, kept Perry out of accidents, and waited for June.

The challenge match began on the first Saturday afternoon of the summer vacation. Originally scheduled at the Governor's House, the site was moved to the Peninsula Hotel on Salisbury Road when His Excellency's staff discovered that there were more persons of color playing than expected. This change of venue did however allow Billy Graham, a chess patzer when he was not converting souls, who was in town for his schedule-crowded first Hong Kong crusade and staying at the same hotel, to watch at least most of the first round before he was ejected from the audience in the final and deciding game played at Board One between Teresa Avila and Paul Klee.

The team and reserves met and decompressed at the rectory of St. Joseph's before taking the short, Number 5 bus-ride to the hotel. In normal clothes instead of our stringent school uniforms, we all looked different to each other, particularly Teresa, stunning in an organdy skirt above brown leather flats and nylons, light brown sleeveless shawl falling from her shoulders and buoyant, white felt hat with a broad brim from which flowed a black flirtation veil. And with the single, seasonal hibiscus pinned to her scapula, she was silent but ready.

At the hotel Pete checked the seeding board and confirmed that our team was indeed last, and the governor's first, in an even field of sixteen. Having consulted the players at the rectory only half an hour ago, and seeing no strategic or seditious necessity to change the board positions at the last minute, he submitted our lineup: Avila, Lopez, Chow, Lombardi, Pluhta, Perry and Rodney.

An overflow crowd had gathered in the main ballroom in which Boards One and Two were to be played on the stage, with manually operated display screens instantly simulating play above the two tables. As the referee announced the conditions of contest, Billy Graham was escorted to his front row seat facing Board One. It seemed obvious that the crowd was excited in anticipation of the blood and carnage to be spilled in the top seed's slaughter of our team. Pete had picked up the Governor's Team's lineup, and knowing the strength of its eight players, we were perplexed by its order. While its strongest player, the Swiss banker and International Master, Paul Klee, was positioned to play at Board One, the strategy of the rest was not obvious: Moritz Rosenthal, John Elway, Lt. William W. Cooke, L. Frank Baum, Ron Guidry, George Gossip, and Alexander Grantham.

Vinnie Lombardi called a fast huddle of the team in an anteroom between ballrooms, *Go for daylight, Go for daylight,* but he was the only one above nervousness to say anything beyond two words.

So on that early June Saturday and Monday while the Day Star, North Star, Shining Star, Morning Star, Meridian Star, Celestial Star, Southern Star, Evening Star, Twinkling Star, and Leading Star sailed across the harbor two hundred and eighty-six times, chess history was made.

On Board Eight, Rodney's early refusal of Grantham's opening Queen's Gambit proved to be costly, allowing the governor to push unrelentingly up the middle. Always on the defensive, she was forced to resign on her twenty-third move, two hours before dinner break. Minus one for us. His Excellency was beaming with gin-and-tonics as he waved his two-fingered victory sign before cameras and reporters in the main lobby. Next day he was quoted in the *South China Morning Post* as saying, *In a crown colony the Governor is next to the Almighty.*

Further disaster hit our team before dinner, at Board Seven in the same ballroom, where Perry had drawn Gossip for his opponent. Drawing black, Gossip had put up a formidable Sicilian Defense. Steady but non-aggressive with his four-hundred-years old opening of pawn to king-four followed by knight to king-bishop-three and bishop to knight-five, Perry slipped on his timing in his fourth move and allowed Gossip, destined to become the worst chess player in the history of the game, to accidentally turn his defense into a king-side offense, forcing a nightmarish mate on the thirty-second move. Minus two for us.

Both Pluhta and Lombardi had better luck with their opponents, Guidry and Baum, on Boards Six and Five in Ballroom C. As white, Pluhta got off to a solid beginning with his King's Gambit, controlling the center with provocative but threatening implications. An early defensive king's-side castling by Guidry on the sixth move put him even further behind. Lombardi threw up a standard French Defense against Baum's Center Pawns' Opening, but on the sixth move, Baum abandoned its conventional continuation and inexplicably pushed his king's-rook-pawn up two squares, a move totally out in the ozone. At the break, both Pluhta and Lombardi were ahead, but the team was still behind, minus two.

In Ballroom B Lindstrom was playing Elway at Board Three, but they appeared to be playing more with each other than the game. A steady flirtation hampered their concentration as Elway followed his well-known motif and practically driveled down the front of Lindstrom's neckline. When he punched the time-clock after his second move, he grinned and said to Lindstrom, *You look very familiar, haven't I met you before,* and after his third move, *You know, you remind me of Ingrid Bergman.* Visibly distracted by this not-so-unwelcomed attention, Lindstrom botched the simple third move of her standard Queen's Gambit opening. From that point on, their games deteriorated. At the break they were tied, in bad moves, and it was anyone's guess how the game could be technically salvaged out of the terminal mess.

At the other table on Board Four in the same ballroom, Lt. Cooke was taking a bath. His premature attack evaporated and Chow encircled the unsupported charge and demolished Cooke's pawn structure and knights as well, in the process gaining both tempo and position. In this all-out slugfest that went only sixteen total moves before the break, eight pieces had been captured. It was clear however, that Chow was way ahead.

On Board Two in the crowded main ballroom, Lopez and Rosenthal were giving a masterpiece exhibition. Rosenthal opened with a Queen's Gambit, and Lopez responded with a deferred Dutch Defense, but on moves four and five pressed his king's-bishop forward for an advantageous bishop exchange. The main lines by both were simple and imaginative, and the balance supportive and flexible. It was clear that the spectators gathered here had come to watch the match on Board One, but by the fifth move, everyone but Billy Graham started paying more attention to the Lopez-Rosenthal board. Before the twenty-third move when Lopez retracted his Queen in his sealed move for the break, the game was very even.

At Board One, the first two moves by Avila and Klee were identical to those by Rosenthal and Lopez at the table forty feet away, but they continued conservatively to the break with no surprises, Avila ever watchful of her verticals, and Klee protective of his horizontals. There was no deviation from the conventional, nothing remarkable, risky or exploitive, only the cautious exploratory, indulgently waiting for the middle game.

—

As we walked to the Jade Garden around the corner from the hotel for a bite to eat, Pete passed out the game records that he had picked up at the scorers' table and gave us his estimated score at the break: ahead in three, even in two, and behind in one, but in the official column, *Minus Two*. Natalie and Bill were mildly apologetic, but they had played their best, and the rest of us appreciated that. Vinnie was ecstatic and, along with the blitzing Don, wanted to have another huddle right there in front of the restaurant on crowded Nathan Road. Pete killed that suggestion when he stopped and looked up from the game record of the Lindstrom-Elway match: *What the hell happened here?*

At dinner, Vinnie's optimism continued, a coachless team seeded last apparently tied with the top seed. Pia and Teresa were silent, though I suspect for very different reasons. It was hard to determine what Teresa was thinking about during dinner, if she was thinking at all. In the only time that she lifted her veil, and that was to drink some water, she looked as if she was in silent meditation. Don was however famished, and after finishing Teresa's plate, started licking his chopsticks.

During the evening session at Board Six where Pluhta was ahead of Guidry at the break, Guidry's sealed move continued to give Pluhta the advantage. But on a surprisingly late king's-side castling followed by a Louisiana-Lightning fast concealed attack on the left verticals, Guidry managed to fight his way back into the game. Not having the time to reorganize his defense, Pluhta could not handle this slider and sought a draw on the thirty-sixth move.

At Board Five across the room, the meaning of Baum's ozoned sixth move became clear. Out of the west, out of the inexplicable pawn to king's-rook sixth move, came everything flying at Lombardi, straw, brick, metal, and a hint of a lion's roar. Ever stigmatic in his horizontals, particularly his pawn structure, Lombardi managed to fend off the attack, but at a devastating cost. Another draw. The score? Still *Minus Two* against us.

Chow was having none of that with Lt. Cooke at Board Four. Cooke's moves after the break suggested that he was obeying someone else's coaching, perhaps Governor Grantham's. They were belligerently aggressive, but they were also self-indulgent, inattentive and disconnected, approaching suicide. After Cooke refused to resign, Chow moved in with his three queens and totally decimated Cooke, leaving no prisoner to be taken. *Plus one, Minus Two,* for a net of *Minus One.*

At the other table on Board Three in the match between Lindstrom and Elway, nothing could be retrieved by either side, and the two of them went down to a dead heat, escaping mate their only consolation, for a net of *Minus One* for the Catholics.

The masterpiece exhibition between Lopez and Rosenthal continued at Board Two in the main ballroom. Everyone's attention was focused on this game, Billy Graham having left at the break to begin his crusade at the racetracks across the harbor in Victoria. As the evening went on, there appeared a certain natural inevitability in the development of Lopez's middle game, against which Rosenthal could only mount an accurate but temporary response. Anticipating the brilliant endgame unfolding as his shared control of center board faltered under Lopez's bifurcated pawn attack, Rosenthal resigned, stood up and graciously congratulated Lopez.

At this point the match was tied between the two teams at ten on a Saturday evening.

Between Avila and Klee at Board One, no strategic advantage had developed. Through their moves and body motions, it was quite obvious that they were cautious and respectful of each other. Both chess analysts in Sunday's *Tiger Standard* and *South China Morning Post* were to use the same word, *patience,* in their descriptions of this game. As it was in the afternoon, their game continued to be simple, unimaginative, but solid, waiting.

Joining the spectators in the main ballroom after his game was over, Pete noticed that Teresa's vertical strength was beginning to be apparent in her king and king's-bishop columns, but he also noticed that she appeared to be either getting nervous or losing stamina, from the way her hands held onto the front ledge of the table. It was approaching midnight however, and Teresa submitted her sealed move to the referee.

Were you getting tired? Pia asked, when Teresa joined us. She had also noticed, but Teresa remained silent behind her black veil.

—

Not wishing to have an accidental leak of her sealed move, we waited until the continuation of the match on Monday morning just before the start of the game to ask Teresa what it was.

I forgot.

Undaunted, Vinnie called a huddle, several sisters and brothers from our schools joining his *Go for daylight.* When we looked up, Billy Graham, the governor and Paul Klee were standing in front of the stage, from which the second table and its simulation screen had been removed. The reverend and governor were smiling and exchanging a hegemonic joke, but Klee only looked distractedly in Teresa's direction for telltale signs.

Wanting an upset now, the spectators were exceptionally noisy as Klee and Avila took their places at Board One while the sealed move was opened and posted on the screen by the steward. Avila stood up to look at her move, studied it in surprise, and then turned to the audience, at once quieting.

Klee took twenty-two minutes to formulate his response, a knight move opening up his horizontal encampment and intended to increase his tempo and initiate some aggression. Avila responded by moving in her chair while her hands rose to grip the table. To everyone's surprise, on her next move she withdrew her pawn protection of her queen's bishop threatened by Klee's last knight move. He looked up at Avila, but decided quickly to capture her bishop, thereby increasing the potential of his attack.

At this point Billy Graham's whistling of Onward Christian Soldiers that coincided with Klee's first aggressive knight move, bothered Klee so much that he asked the referee to eject the reverend from the game. After the ensuing unsuccessful protest by both Grantham and Graham had subsided, Avila made another surprise move by exposing her other bishop. Klee looked up at her again, searching for a design, and just as quickly while she gripped the edge of the table, captured it, leaving her bishopless.

Now lifting one foot off the floor, Avila moved her knight to threaten Klee's king's-rook, at the same time disclosing a queen king-check. Three consecutive brilliant moves in a row, sacrificing her two bishops for a disclosed check that will at least achieve a draw. But both of her feet were off the floor now. The audience was speechless. Avila was clearly beginning to levitate while she was hanging on to the table. Klee's mouth was open, and as Avila rose higher and higher and the edge of the table started to tremble, his hands too reached out for the table and gripped it to hold it down. But it was futile. The table was tipped, the chess pieces, clocks, pencils and paper pads and water glasses all tumbled onto the stage as Avila went upwards, upwards until she was stopped by the proscenium arch.

Governor Grantham and the referee were the first to get up on stage, with the governor insisting that Teresa come down instantly, this very minute. But His Almighty was Protestant, Church of England, and by now the sisters and brothers had their crucifixes out and were kneeling on the ballroom floor in deep prayer. The cameramen who were not allowed into the ballroom now went up to the skirt of the stage and started flashing their bulbs; some of the reporters took notes while others dashed to the phones out in the main lobby.

Slowly, so slowly that her organdy skirt did not even balloon, Teresa descended. Klee walked over to help her down, bowed and closed his eyes.

This is outrageous, This is a sacrilege to the game, shouted His Excellency as he demanded our team's forfeiture. We had little choice. Things were too out of control.

—

On the hotel's promenade, in the bright sunlight of an early June in Hong Kong on that Monday morning, Teresa said to us, *We didn't win, it's not my fault,* as if after what happened winning was still an issue with us; but she smiled and added for all of us, *We'll never play like this again.*

It was a story that drew all of us into a magical event whose remembrance would stay with each one of us for the rest of our lives. And as we said our *Good-byes* to each other, we also knew then that we would probably never see each other again.

THE READER'S PURGE KIT

Through the indiscretion of bright words that inform our dreamscapes, we are pushed to the limits of our patience or imagination, depending on our mood. But we do know that as long as we continue to confront such explorations, we cannot die, lest the story continue without us. It was at first awakening that this promise burst in, disquieting, an unmistakable reality, but it was ours. Then as we are swamped by our tedious complications — cooking, sleeping, counting — our histories become diminished, and we are left at the end gazing blankly at the sidewalks and front yards of other people's faces wondering if we are all looking at the same things without mercy. The denial of historical accuracy and assault on simple good taste have brought us this story with its bizarre metaphoric implications, as well as necessitating this questionable consolation. The author will however send you a xeroxed hand-record of the games when he receives your request and SASE, if that is the only way you have of approaching truth.

The Great Wall, Al, Flo, Zeke And $\Delta\Delta M$

Having been in Beijing for less than thirty-six hours, he boarded a van headed northwest out of the inner city to tour the Great Wall with three other Americans, teachers assigned to Beijing Forestry University. The countryside was mostly agricultural along the one-hour drive up a mountain highway to Badaling, the North Pass at a strategic divide.

Over the last thirty-five years, the Central Committee of the Party, the ruling unit within the central government, developed several national plans to feed its peoples and make the nation self-sufficient in food production. The segment of the plan that applied to Beijing, China's capital, as well as most other Chinese cities, mandated that these individual municipalities in turn be self-sufficient in their food supply. As a consequence, Beijing city planners limited industrial growth, halted new heavy industry, and shifted to autonomous food production even as the city continued to sprawl outwards at an alarming rate. Of the 9.5 million people living in this area the size of Belgium and larger than Connecticut, 42 percent of its population is tied to agriculture. Strips of mostly deciduous trees, willows, poplars and other fast growing softwoods, formed corridors separating the highway from the farms which, in that early September, were harvesting a wide assortment of melons, grapes, apples, pears, corn, squashes, zucchini, waxed beans, peppers, potatoes, and tomatoes. Cattle and sheep grazed the hillsides, and hogs and chickens bivouacked at every bricked farmhouse, however small.

Horse-drawn carts transporting produce south and building materials north competed with the Mazda for use of the highway. As in the inner city itself, there appeared the non-ending development and construction activity all along and away from the highway. The obvious oversupply of labor seemed to be delicately balanced against random mechanization and automation. Individual workers appeared intent on small and isolated projects of independent labor with no apparent connection to any larger geography or organizational plan, an image difficult to visualize in Japan.

But somehow the jobs get done, always, the connections made, with or without the plumb line. Like the downtown traffic where there exists no regulation for the operation of cars, buses, trolleys, bicycles, farm tractors, trucks and pedestrians, (except that those with wheels mostly used the right side of the streets and were generally attentive to the few traffic lights most of the time, and individuals arrived at the destination of their choice with fewer headaches, curses and accidents than their compatriot residents in Los Angeles, Rome, London, or Tokyo) the users of this mountain highway were equally attentive to each other's space and movements while staying in constant motion themselves.

On an occasional bridge stood a solitary soldier helmeted and armed with an AK-47/S at white-gloved, port-arms position, his stare fixed at a frozen object over one's shoulder. His uniform was shaded the same green as Beijing's city police, its epaulets and shoulder patches differentiating their purpose and function. Their presence on these bridges seemed to reflect more particularly a

Sandhurst perimeter containment mentality than a modern political philosophy.

At Badaling, the recently expanded northern city limits of Beijing, there were no soldiers or police (except as tourists themselves) guarding the Great Wall that, according to some historians, was an idealization to keep out invaders from the north. That the wall itself has actually kept anyone out, or in, is highly debatable, although dissident intellectuals tend to see it as a geographical symbol of internal oppression and cultural isolation. Legend has it that if and when The Wall is to fall, as sections of it did during the Cultural Revolution when the People's Liberation Army tore it down to recycle the bricks for barracks construction, the last soldiers will be instructed to send up smoke signals from treated wolf dung so that the turret guards at the Imperial Palace some 45 kilometers south in the center of Beijing can prepare themselves for some serious combat. Legend also has it that in the first three centuries of the modern calendar, unwanted residents from the inner city were expelled through these gates at Badaling to face the *wolves of the terrifying wild west*. Modern legend records that The Wall is the only human edifice visible from the moon.

Reading about these legends in guide books had not prepared him for what he encountered. White Mice augmented the tiny set of traffic lights at the narrow baluster which is itself part of The Wall, directing the constant flow of Toyotas, Peugeots, Mercedes, Red Flags, Volgas and even some ancient Morris Minors through the north-south portal. The pigeons that have almost entirely disappeared from Beijing because of an extensive extermination program that seemed to have strayed to include other small birds by accident as well, now reappeared suddenly on the rooftops and building ridges north of The Wall, just as the trained homing pigeons that learned the political significance of the 28th Parallel and North Panmunjom and South Panmunjom during the Korean War truce talks at the border could tell discrete, arbitrary geographical differences. More than humans, they knew where home was, then as well as now.

The Wall itself was built onto a ridgeback that appeared humanly not scaleable from both approaches in most sections around Badaling. Started some 2,500 or 2,700 years ago, depending which historian one talks to, more than a million pairs of hands and feet gave of their labor to its construction. At its initial stages before the advent of the modern calendar, those workers who died at this site, presumably prisoner-slaves, unwittingly also contributed their other body parts as building material. During the Ming Dynasty, when Europe was trying to decide if Earth was round or flat or both and some actually ventured out to prove or disprove it or both, most of The Wall was refaced with stone and brick. Before and after this period, its history is blurry, as obscure as its real function and whatever else its metaphor may have represented in the Chinese imagination, as well as ours.

Today the government itself advertises The Wall as one of the world's greatest tourist attractions. And indeed, the only modernized cross-cultural tourist feature missing at this border site was access for the handicapped. There was piped music wired along sections of The Wall around Badaling. The public toilets attended to by minority tribal teenagers collecting the five-fen user fee stood next to stores selling Great Wall postcards, *I climbed the Great Wall* t-shirts, Great Wall ashtrays, Great Wall satin pillows, Great Wall scarves, 1985 and 1989 Great Wall calendars hanging side by

Great Wall side. There were also camels on which one could sit for Polaroid pictures, and ermine pelts at bargain price. Most of the tourists ventured west or east from Badaling, and some both.

Either direction is a climb, however, the western segment gaining some 400 meters in less than one kilometer. Most visitors seemed prepared with cameras, binoculars, water jugs, and for some, even four-course lunches with beer and fruit. It was odd that such organizing principles also included wearing suit and tie, volleyball uniform with Nike Air Jordans, spiked heels, legal briefcases, and a singularly beautiful older Mongolian woman with a long, deep-blue native skirt with braided red trim interrupting this cognitive dissonance. She did not take notice of the young lovers on holiday from Shanghai snapping each other's picture on the high parapet in their matching Reeboks, but continued in her effortless stride up the steepest section of The Wall.

Stretched out 2,400 kilometers against an ecosystem of black pines, yews, sub-alpine spruces, dwarf oaks, mountain maples and white-spotted pines, The Wall must be the ultimate dream surface for the graffiti junkie. Only recently have the authorities begun a campaign to discourage graffiti art and smoking on The Wall. Most of the writing is in Chinese, but an occasional English or German word would appear. The first that caught his eye was *AL,* in four inch block capitals. Then many steps later, *FLO.* Then *ZEKE.* Then *ΔΔΜ,* which he had to guess represented all the sisters in the Delta Delta Mu sorority at the University of Michigan. Then another *AL.* Perhaps it was carved by the same Al or same Al's girlfriend some 500 steps apart, or perhaps it was by another Al or his girlfriend, or perhaps it was by the first Al who had come up for a second visit and had forgotten that he had already cut his name into a brick on his previous trip.

The fixed trope here is, of course, picture taking. Of each other mostly, and just maybe one frame left for the backdrop, the scenery, the landscape, depending on how one looked at it. There were four cameras in his group of five, taking each other's pictures in various planned and random combinations. Such a camera stop took up at least ten full minutes. It was fortunate that he had not brought a camera along, since he calculated that an additional camera in the group would have inserted at least seven more minutes into each camera summons.

The preferred pose while having one's picture taken at The Wall appeared to be perpetual detente. While courtesy seemed to be a rare encounter in Beijing's inner city as it is in all other large cities, here in the high altitude, every possible courtesy is extended to the process of every individual picture being prepared and shot. No one, just no one, not even children, ventured into someone else's focal plane, regardless of how long it took to wait. If one listened carefully, one would have heard the three most frequently used words: *Yi, er, camera!*

On the way down he walked with one of the Educational Services Exchange with China teachers who was also taking notes. He found out that she was fundamentalist Christian, a recent master's-in-education recipient from the University of Virginia, who was in Beijing for the year to teach English to China's future foresters through the non-denominational, emphasized *non-*denominational, church organized and funded ESEC. She said that this tour had been the happiest moment of her life, as she was able to experience history or myth, as he supposed one did by touring Manassas outside Charlottesville or Little Big Horn or Minidoka. Modern legend has it that the former chairman Mao had said, *If you don't make it to The Wall, you're not a Chinese.* Deconstructed by this member of the interdenominational God-Squadder and applied to its mission, it meant, *Let's visit the Great Wall to see what being Chinese is all about,* whose subtext of course read, *Let me learn to love the Chinese, Lord.*

It is an ironic turn on this ultimate symbol of tyranny, that the individual lens can turn Earth's most visible matrix between order and chaos, good and evil, and incidentally, light and dark, as in ethnicity, into a delusionary experiencing of history just by being there for three hours, one of them spent squandering color nitrates. There may well have been human history here, some twenty-four or twenty-seven centuries of it, and he supposed it was even happening then; but he didn't think that this was the kind of text that will be included in someone's focal plane, regardless of how long they stop to take pictures. For him, the moment has come to mean a collapsed sequence on seeing, after his descent, a facsimile of his burgundy Jeep Cherokee in the parking lot. For him, the moment has come to mean the tall Mongolian lady in blue visiting this matrix that was drawn to keep out her kin.

The Answer

They are the pictographs from five thousand years.
They are the watchful eyes of future generations.
— Bei Dao

Less then a week ago he was leaving Troy on his horse. The sentry at the gates stopped him and reminded him that he could not leave town, horses were not permitted to leave. So he left his horse and started his 9,385 miles journey by car. Less than a week ago he had not known Xiaohong existed, when life in Idaho was simpler and decisions rarely involved consequences. But now the two of them were bicycling across the city to meet her friend who would take him to a piano that he could play at the National Conservatory of Music. That only a week ago he should read in the paper of the 58-8 defeat of Troy's first football game of the season was an accident, for he was not looking for it, but merely taking a departing glance at the local news before saddling up his horse for his trip to the airport.

Xiaohong waited until he cycled alongside, then asked "How do I get to your graduate university?

"What do you mean?"

"Do I have to take the TOEFL test?

"Yes, I think so; I've heard it mentioned."

"TOEFL is stupid, it's not a good language test."

They had to split up again to pass a farmer bringing his fall harvest of potatoes and cauliflower into town on his horsedrawn cart. It was all right to bring horses into Beijing. The night before he left, he had gone with friends to watch that first eight-man football game under Troy's new head coach. Troy received the kickoff in the rain, but it was only after Highlander, ranked number one in the state in its class, had scored two touchdowns and two successful conversions that Troy gained its first yardage.

They parked their bicycles at the gate to the music school and headed for the graduate apartments, where Xiaohong introduced him to her boyfriend Luojun, a student in musicology. Inside the one-room apartment, he was further introduced to Luojun's three roommates and invited to join their six-course lunch with wine and beer and nuts and moon-cakes celebrating the autumn harvest festival. After declining a penalty, Highlander took possession of the ball, and its wily quarterback, deceptively adept at the option play, passed again for another touchdown and another conversion.

"You cannot play here," Luojun said, "only students can play here. But we find a way."

He continued to outline the scheme. The wily quarterback was equally spectacular on defense, a free safety who read every play, whose inescapable tackles terrorized the entire backfield. When the team and its boosters boarded the school buses for the odyssey back to Winchester and Craigmont, did he have to leave his horse at the gate?

"You learn some Chinese and, and, be student here and play."

"And yes?"

"And I will unlock room with piano."

"I'll be teaching in Beijing for four months." he held up four fingers with his right hand. "Can I practice three times a week?" he asked, changing the number of fingers. The score kept on changing; the more it rained, the more Highlander scored. He left his friends in the rain and went home to pack for his trip before the first quarter was over.

"Yes."

"Tuesdays, Thursdays, and Saturdays at two o'clock?"

"Okay. You come to my room first, then I take you to piano." Then looking at him without smiling this time, Luojun continued. "If you have trouble, you no know me. I am not friend. I have no key to piano room. Now you eat with us?"

Unlike most of the people at Troy, he thought, Xiaohong's friends are not trapped: they are covered, they have it both ways. In Troy crimes are rare, but when they occur they are severe and sometimes terminal, murdering a friend since kindergarten and fishing partner, or a father's sexual abuse of his daughters. Between crimes they still use hounds to hunt black bear, and the farmers and growers continue to demand and receive reparation from the state for deer and elk damage to their crops and orchards. The landscape has not altered their lives even as they continue to master it with their indiscriminate chainsaws and political dams: in success or failure, almost all continue to be living embellishments to the spirit of mobility and frontier individualism, and as such, as they approach the twenty-first century as never before, they have not accepted any responsibility for it.

Not so with Luojun and his friends, he thought. They have been politically liberated but they have circumvented their responsibility by keeping their personal options loose. Like the parable about language and fact, in which the *white horse* is challenged if it's a horse or an emperor or C.O., rather than, if it's white; here if Luojun plants melon seeds, will he get melons? Is eight-man football football?

—

On the next Saturday he rode his black-hulk Flying Pigeon to the music school where Luojun let him into a practice room and left him alone to a piano. He sat down at the Tsanghai upright and started Bach's E minor partita, but he could not get into it, nor next into Mozart's D minor concerto — the sound wasn't right, he wasn't making music, only correct but disconnected notes on a piano. In Troy several months ago when he was studying with his first good teacher, these pieces were beginning to come together, and for the first time in his life he felt he was making music happen. Most people he knew in Troy didn't particularly want to be there, just as they didn't want to be particularly anywhere else either. Where they lived in Troy and how they lived, their values did not change, but they did not feel they were in any real trouble, and some even lived to die there. But that was not the case with his teacher who wanted to be particularly somewhere else and would leave for it instantly, and did, without any more trauma than turning a page of the newspaper. If given the opportunity to return and visit, he definitely would decline.

About the time his teacher left town, he was making final plans to leave himself for a semester of teaching in Beijing, passport, visa, plane reservations, leave request, AIDS test, entrusting his finances and horse to his best friend. Now he was pretending to be a Chinese student at the National Conservatory of Music in Beijing practising maybe three times a week after promising to allege fraud and deny culpability if discovered.

After a sharp metallic knock at the door in the middle of the rondo of the D minor, someone unlocked the door and entered, a woman in a janitorial-blue blazer and short hair with a large ring filled with room keys. She was a lady in control of her own future, and immediately started asking questions in Chinese. He couldn't understand most of it, and at first just shook his head, but as she persisted in raising her voice and ringing power from her keys he felt he had to say something.

"*Wu bu dong,*" were the only words that came to him intuitively, but they were not good enough for her, nor was his getting up from the piano bench and taking an equal step away from it and her.

This superintendent of questions raised her voice some more, and he could tell from the little Chinese he knew that she was beginning to repeat the whole series of questions again. Just from the strident tone of her voice and her finger pointing to him, to the piano, to the door-lock, and then to him again, he knew that she felt personally assaulted by someone she didn't know had dared to use one of her pianos, that she was challenging his authenticity as a music student at the conservatory, that she was asking how he got a key for this locked practice room.

He remembered hearing about a high-school exchange student, an Erica Voxman from West Germany, whose favorite pastime was going shopping at the big mall in Moscow fifteen miles from Troy. It was at that point that he decided he would like to spend some time away from Troy, and started making inquiries about a visiting appointment in China, the birthplace of his parents. And now he was here, and his interrogator would not be put off by his silence.

"Wo shi Meiguo ren," he said, and reached into his wallet to show her his Idaho driver's license that included a photograph of him but not his horse. *"Wo shi Meiguo ren,"* he repeated, pointing to his color photograph and then to himself.

A faint whisper of a smile appeared in her eyes as she peered down at his photograph in recognition, but just as suddenly it disappeared as she started into her series of questions again, her keys jangling, the quarterback passing again for another abusive two-point conversion.

At another pause, he tried again. *"Wo shi Meiguo ren: wo bu dong."*

"Meiguo ren. Ah, Meiguo ren," she repeated, and left the room but instantly reappeared, bringing with her a man about her age who must have been listening around the corner.

"Meiguo ren," she said, pointing to him, and again launched into her series of questions which by now were beginning to sound like accusations.

At this point, the man looked at the Idaho driver's license and said "American," but this appeared to be the extent of his English vocabulary.

The ruckus was beginning to attract others, and soon there were eight persons tucked into the small practice room, now nine, counting the one without his horse. At the entrance of each new person, the lady with the keys exploded into her litany of questions. Each of the newcomers would introduce one or two new English words, but together they could not pull them into a sentence or question that could be understood, especially when they were all speaking at the same time. The last time he felt this vulnerable happened this spring after he had been fishing with two children who were very successful with their catch but negligent in their addition, when the uniformed and armed game warden stopped them to check their day's limit. Here there were no uniforms: some were faculty from their better clothes and polished leather shoes, and some students from their younger age; but both appeared to be masking threats, guarding against a seedy counter-revolutionary usurpation of property rights.

After repeated moments of silence that waited expectantly for him to say something had passed, everyone left suddenly, shutting the door behind them, except for the one who had said nothing throughout, who looked somewhere between a faculty and student.

"Please sit," he said calmly, pointing to the piano bench, the only place in the room a person could sit. "She go to bring English teacher."

The man without his horse could not understand his earlier silence, could not read the meaning of why he waited until everyone had left before he said anything, in English or Chinese. But most of all, he did not know how much trouble he was in, if the incident was over, or if this was just an intermission.

During furtive moments, the two men looked carefully at each other.

"Are you a student here?" the man without the horse tried to find a resolution to his dilemma, taking the upper hand.

"No, I am teacher."

"What do you teach?"

"Piano. Your Bach is very good. I listened," he said, and picked up the score of Copland's piano sonata, reading it carefully.

"*Xie, xie.*"

The lady with the keys returned with a serious-looking man with thick glasses who introduced himself as Mr. He Fang Ming, the English teacher, but he did not offer to shake hands.

"How did you get in?" he asked, and "Why are you here?"

"I'm teaching in Beijing," the man without his horse said, and gave Mr. He his business card. "I am an American, a teacher from Idaho. I also play the piano. A friend said I could find a piano at your school to practise on."

"Who let you into this locked room?"

"No one. I found it unlocked."

"She says this room is always locked. But no matter, you cannot play piano here; only our students can play piano here." In a different language, he was saying the same things as the lady with the keys. "You come to my room. We talk."

He gathered his music and the two of them walked wordless up a flight of stairs and into the English teacher's room. Since he was bigger, the man without his horse thought momentarily about bolting, of running out and vaulting onto his horse for an escape, but he also knew that it would be hopeless, that with a horse he would most certainly be stopped at the gates.

In his room, Mr. He closed the door and said, "Please, sit."

There was a knock at the door and Luojun appeared and said something to Mr. He in Chinese.

"He is student here," Mr. He explained, "and he heard commotion downstairs. He come to see."

Luojun also sat down and then said something else in Chinese to Mr. He, the only person still standing.

"He said he let you into piano room," Mr. He said and waited, but the man without his horse and his bicycle was absolutely speechless at Luojun's admission of complicity, his reading of fact totally scrambled, as he and Luojun shared the same destiny, if only for a few seconds. "But no matter, I will talk with director, find out if you can play piano here."

"Thank you very much."

"Not important. Is this your Beijing telephone number here on your card?"

"Yes."

"I will telephone you and let you know what answer is."

"Thank you."

"You may have to pay."

After their good-byes, he left the building, checking his bike at the gate, and discretely noted that it had taken him exactly one week to get here from Troy.

Progeny

But if I find them, do I beat the kid?
Do I beat the father? Do I beat the teacher?

— Israel Ben-Avraham

When he was born in October of 1953 in Berkeley, his parents named him Hillary with an extra *l*. Now he is back teaching in Beijing and making more money than he thinks he should. He still worries about it every day bicycling to class and around the city, but not as much as when he used to ride past the small group of mud huts housing the workers on campus. More than the thirty-six years of his body, he has learned to recognize poverty when he sees it, now huddled around these recent ethnic emigrants, at least three generations hunkered down by the side of their cooking pots in the dark, *fanhes* in hand for their only meal of the day, tattered and waiting.

One lunch at the dormitory's crowded cafeteria more than two months ago, he saw one of these men working as a cook. A student in front of him demanded more rice at the window counter, but the cook refused, banging his spoon down on the rice for emphasis. Someone yelled *da,* echoed by another *da,* and the cook threw down his spoon this time and rushed out at the student, rolling up his sleeves and followed by four other cooks shaking their spatulas. The five of them crouched and mimed around the student, when suddenly they all jumped at him at once, pummeling him with their spatulas. Just as suddenly and before anyone could interfere, the fighting stopped, and the illusion of civility resumed with the diminishing yells.

That night as Hillary caught the faint odor of wood smoke drifting from the cooking fires while he stood smoking on his veranda in the dark, he decided what he wanted to do with his excessive salary. He waited until the fires were out and, sure that they had abandoned their day, he took 10 *yuan* from his dresser and went downstairs. Working his way very carefully without a flashlight, he followed the dirt path to the cook's hut, and, when he was near enough, left the money under a small rock.

At breakfast the next morning, Hillary queued up in this cook's line to get a closer look, and, knowing better, tried to see something different, and did not. But he felt different, and it showed in his classes, a shielded happiness that would not let go. That afternoon he rode his bicycle to the Central Academy of Fine Arts where he cancelled his tentative painting purchases. He had been in Beijing long enough to know not to offer any explanations for it, and so he wasn't asked for any. It was a deliberate simplification in a country that cultivated diminutive elaborations within colossal masks.

The landscape painter continued to tutor him on traditional painting, this lesson emphasizing the importance of the artist's personal seal, the final addition before a work is considered finished. His own paintings of the mountains between Tibet and Nepal showed three seals, the last one stamped near the identical tallest peak in each, and with them, he told Hillary about the heritage that had been passed down one generation of artists to the next in the seals. Hillary noticed it was also here where the snow gathered itself against the seals, that his namesake had made his historical ascent.

For more than a month he continued to leave some money at the entrance to the cook's hut, at least once a week. He looked carefully for changes every day when he bicycled past these mud huts and at the cafeteria window, but the children who never went to school continued to look after their younger siblings in the same clothes, their parents continued to work twelve hours a day, seven days a week, and the smoke from the fires warming the gruel and cabbage continued to rise only once a day.

Two weeks ago in the TOEFL class in which Hillary was coaching students to pass the language test as one of the many requirements for a select few to study in the United States, his best student in the class stopped all discussion when she challenged their motivation, accusing them of running away from their motherland and not intending to return, accusing them of pursuing selfish and materialistic lives instead of helping their country modernize and compete effectively in the next century. A long silence followed her outburst as the other students looked to Hillary to get the class back on track, but his sympathies were with her, an older student whose teacher-parents had been sent to a rural western province for ideological rehabilitation during the Cultural Revolution, leaving her with her grandparents when she was eleven, and has since used that experience as a fulcrum for balancing her life and its relevance. Refusing to budge from her position, she and the TOEFL coach pursued a discussion in which she argued that both the Cultural Revolution and the recent Tiananmen Square incident were the inevitable historical imperatives of the masses, an absolute tyranny anticipated by de Tocqueville when he observed the birth of the United States but now equally applicable to the People's Republic of China 150 years later; and he took the view that the Cultural Revolution led by Jiang Qing was the ultimate women's revenge on a society that had cruelly and systematically oppressed them for more than forty-two centuries. Hillary learned later that several of the male students had complained to the department leader in a symbolic gesture of criticism, accusing him of failing as a teacher because he was always late for his classes.

Later that same night Hillary took the dirt path to the cook's hut to leave some more money but, being distracted by the TOEFL class discussion, he did not notice that he was earlier than usual, and the cook was waiting for him at the side of the hut's entrance. Caught in the act of covering the bill with a rock, he could not feign any illusion, mask or symbol, but resorted to shrugging his shoulders silently.

Though he could not understand the cook's heavy ethnic dialect, Hillary knew from his tone that the cook was angry, and caught enough to understand *foreigner* and *betrayal*, and *never, never* repeated several times. As he continued to shrug his shoulders, the cook called his family from their hut. Standing there in the near-dark he asked each of the adults to empty their pockets of their money, and in a ritual they collectively crumpled and threw the bills and coins at Hillary's feet before returning to their hut, leaving him staring at the embers in the late fire.

When he got back to his apartment, he picked up his telephone to call his parents in California, just to know if they were still there, and if the line was still working. Since then he has learned to avoid these mud huts, to take the long way around to his classroom building and the post office, and to stand in a different line for his meals at the cafeteria. Occasionally in the early morning hours, Hillary would be awakened by the sound of the cook lightly clinking a piece of hollow piping against a brick, rhythmically reminding him of where he was exactly; and some other nights he would wake up startled, listening intently for this sinking noise that wasn't there.

Flowers

It had all been carefully arranged. In the capital for just ten days to attend a conference, Wangli wanted to spend his only free day to meet Shen Peng, a calligrapher-poet whose work he had admired from his distant western province of Qinghai. So he made the appropriate excuses to pass up the conference-tour of the Imperial Palace and the Great Wall at Badaling, and instead made his own separate arrangements through a mutual friend. He would first meet this Yuying at the Tiananmen Square post office at exactly one o'clock; then they would ride their bicycles to the eastern gates of the Central Academy of Fine Arts to meet Xiao-an, a former student of Shen Peng's. Though now a recognized artist in her own right, after gaining a toe-hold in the capital's men-dominated tough art circles for having designed and executed several large outdoor porcelain murals, Xiao-an figured into these arrangements only because the master-teacher Shen Peng would not grant interviews to a stranger. To assure an appointment, Wangli had to pretend that he was related to Xiao-an, in fact her distant cousin. Xiao-an, a friend of Yuying's, was then the friend-of-a-friend of Wangli's, but as his illusionary cousin, she was the person who opened the door for him to meet Shen Peng. Yuying was then their go-between, and would also serve as the translator should any of them fail to communicate with each other in their regional accents. This is the way things still are in Beijing, the capital of modern China.

At exactly one o'clock on this first October Sunday, Wangli looked for Yuying in front of the post office by Tiananmen Square. She had promised over the phone that he would recognize her for wearing a yellow windbreaker, an unusual clothing color, although at this time of year, potted yellow and red chrysanthemums proliferated on every avenue and in front of every public building in the capital. Bicyclists wearing jackets of all colors except yellow sped by him, bells ringing. Dizzied by this traffic, Wangli sought escape by envisioning his hometown, a small provincial city at the foot of a high mountain, where life seemed more tranquil and less trivialized. But here he has noticed that even the occasional cats and dogs he's seen have adopted this human pattern, a goal-intense behavior muffled within a four-legged fright. But before Wangli could extrapolate any reverse-anthropomorphic significance out of this comparison, a yellow blur whizzed by him, accompanied by a bicycle bell's loud jingling.

After their self-introductions, Yuying and Wangli joined the bicycle traffic and rode east on the wide Chang An Avenue to meet Xiao-an, who would then introduce them to Shen Peng. At Tiananmen Square a company of soldiers with AK-47s still stood guard, their rigid attention warning the public to keep off. Wangli kept his head down, his eyes focused on the cement and cobbled surfaces, looking for some remaining sign of the recent violence. As he slowed down for a more careful scrutiny, he could feel and hear the oppressed breathing of a tattered worker passing on his right, the wheels of his trailer-bicycle the only thing that kept him from being bent under the crushing weight of his life. A civil engineer, Wangli thought that this was how far we've come in forty years, after all, and pressed down to catch up with Yuying's yellow dot in the distance.

Xiao-an was waiting for them at the art school's east entrance. She was wearing a white duster, and the advertised, tinted Elton John glasses, some impatience showing through her smiling introductions that Wangli could not understand at all. Yuying explained that Xiao-an had spent her childhood outside Ulaanbaatar with her brother after their father was killed by the Red Guards roaming through the streets one night, making their mother mad and incapable of taking care of even herself. Consequently, Xiao-an identified herself with the Inner Mongolian in language and culture, and on special occasions would wear her traditional sea-blue dress with full skirt trimmed in thick red braids, and boots and wide belt. Through Yuying, Xiao-an asked Wangli not to betray their conspiracy, and should the Master Shen inquire about the details of their relationship, their grandfathers were brothers would be the correct answer. He thought that it was beginning to get out of hand, originally a simple and innocent deceit now involving Red Guards, Mongolians storming across the Great Wall in white dusters and United Nations interpreters in amnesty yellow. He wanted to bolt, to get away from these two women who had been strangers to him until only a few moments ago, and were now even stranger, to jump onto his borrowed bicycle and return to his hotel room to wait for the next conference session, to save Shen Peng's poems and writings to be studied privately and without complications at home, safely tucked away in remote western China. But it was too late for that now; having come this far, Wangli had to see it through.

139

The three of them walked their bicycles past the gatekeepers, and parked them in front of a walled, small courtyard. A gentle man who looked like he never took a nap, the Master Shen Peng came out and met them, and appeared genuinely glad to see them all, particularly Wangli, who had come more than 5,000 *li* from the high mountains of the west. Ever alert about his manners, Wangli profusely thanked the master for having been such a good teacher to his cousin and for helping her with her career in Beijing.

Inside his spacious studio lined with postcards sent to him from all over the world from his former students, and traditional landscape paintings and calligraphy done in different inks and with every imaginable brush and pen, Shen Peng prepared tea for the four of them. Noting Wangli's hometown, Shen withdrew from a bookshelf a large pictorial book carefully wrapped in protective paper.

"This is a new book I edited, with photographs from all over China. Here, here is one of your hometown."

Wangli looked at the pictures, amazed that the photographer was able to take such a revealing photograph of his city looking into the light of a setting sun, the city itself receding into the deep colors at the foot of the tall mountain, and in the distance, the two becoming inseparable. Then he saw the photographer's credit on the bottom of the page, *Shen Peng.* He turned to the cover of the book, *Shen Peng* again. He had no idea that the master calligrapher-poet also edited books and was a landscape photographer as well. Inside the dust cover, Wangli found his other credentials: Member of Standing Committee of All China Association of Literature and Art, Vice-Chairman of Chinese Calligraphers' Association, Vice-Director of Theory Committee — Chinese Artists Association, Assistant Editor in Chief of People's Fine Arts Publishing House, Chief Editor of *Chinese Calligraphy and Painting*, and now Professor of Calligraphy, Central Academy of Fine Arts.

To keep him from acting dumfounded, Shen Peng said, "Come to my desk, I want to make something for you."

The three of them watched the master prepare the ink, and after quickly selecting a brush from among the hundreds in the stands on his writing desk, Shen proceeded to write a poem on a piece of scrolled paper in a controlled freehand while standing up over his desk. Wangli's mouth opened in amazement. He had always admired Shen's work, both the poems as well as the writing, having often acquired a way of managing his life from them. Shen's work had played such a crucial role in his life, particularly through the decade of aberration, that Wangli wanted to meet him. Just to see him getting off a bus would have been enough, but this was something else, the master was writing a poem for him right in front of his very eyes. Shen's strokes flowed easily from his brush, nuances of black ink emerging on the paper into blossoms of meaning, radicalizing its whorls, turns and pedicels into everlasting visual memory.

Nothing in life is fully perfect
From its bold beginning
To its tentative end — in your hands
In mine, in ours all —
It is slightly imperfect
But we look for perfection
Such is our hope, our dream, our peace

Our Nelson and Winnie Mandellas

To the measured left of the last line, Shen added the dedication, signed and dated it, and, very carefully unwrapping three jade stamps, he inked them, breathed onto them, and firmly applied their seals onto the poem.

By this time Xiao-an had walked over to Wangli's side and put her arm around his waist. His attention directed at the master's work, he was first not aware that a woman's arm was about his waist; but as he started out of habit to remove it with his hand, he remembered their stated relationship, and wondering that maybe in this part of China cousins were supposed to put their arms about each other, he stopped, but not before her fingers had locked onto his behind his back. This he knew wasn't, so he tried to extricate himself by moving closer to the table, slowly and surreptitiously so as not to attract any attention, not to blow the identity-cover, at last getting loose.

Wangli was dizzy again, first because, as used as he was to the custom of reciprocal gift-giving — which he often interpreted as a self-serving rule of give-unto-others-first-so-that-they-will-therefore-owe-you-and-give-to-you-more-in-return — it was obvious that Shen wanted nothing from him in return; then because he could not interpret the meaning of Xiao-an's move; but mostly because he felt deeply embarrassed for having fabricated a lie in order to meet Shen, this overwhelming and extravagant poet. Totally unsettled now, Wangli was barely aware of anything more until they left Shen's studio.

In the fresh air now, Shen accompanied them as far as the outside gate, before their final good-byes. At Chang An Avenue in rush hour, Xiao-an yelled something to Wangli and Yuying before her white duster disappeared entirely into the roiling bicycle traffic in the opposite direction.

"What did she say?" Wangli yelled over the din of bicycle bells and car horns.

". . . and asked 'How much in life is enough?'"

"What?"

"How much is enough? enough?"

Wangli tried to reconstruct the sentence in his ear, but he could only remember his father once saying as the two of them walked through the winter streets of his secluded hometown many years ago, "If you have to ask it, you have too much." He had never understood its meaning until now.

—

During the conference noon-break on Tuesday, Wangli received a call from Yuying.

"You're not here?"

"No. I am here at the conference."

"Xiao-an will be here in a few minutes."

Wangli was confused. He wanted to say *so?*, but instead *huh?* involuntarily came out of his mouth.

"She has rearranged her art classes this afternoon so that she can meet with you. You forgot?"

Wangli was now totally confused. "Forgot what?"

"You said you wanted to see her again, this afternoon, at my room, and she has prepared some Mongolian food for you."

Wangli was beginning to panic. No I didn't he said to himself, but he wasn't entirely sure, so he only managed, "I don't remember." The phone went silent but he could tell they were not disconnected. So he added, "I'm sorry; I don't ever remember."

"Can you come down now?"

"No I can't — I have to make this afternoon's presentation," and as if to legitimate his reason, he added, "on the impact of rail and bus travel on highland populations."

"She will be disappointed," Yuying said, and Wangli thought that she sounded more concerned than a disinterested translator would, her pencil gripped too firmly in hand, ferociously taking notes lest she left anything out.

"Then you will call and explain to her? I can't."

Wangli hesitated, then after a long pause, said, "Hello? Hello?"

"Yes?"

"Okay, in a few minutes then. But how can I talk to her when we speak different languages?"

"There's an extension here — I'll translate."

"In a moment then."

Wangli went back to his room, and for the few minutes he had to himself, imagined the picture of Xiao-an in her white duster and tinted Elton John glasses astride her mare in full gallop over some high Mongolian plain, daring the most eligible bachelor to pull in her reins in violent courtship.

—

This was Xiano-an now, whose father was beaten to death one night by roughshod teenagers wandering through the neighborhood defining *trouble,* on the phone in a dialect Wangli couldn't decipher.

"Yes? I'm here," Yuying assured Wangli.

Xiao-an said something that Yuying did not translate.

"I'm sorry I absolutely forgot about today." Wangli again, "How about tomorrow afternoon?" knowing full well that Xiao-an could not possibly change her schedule on such short notice.

Yuying added a perfunctory *No,* but Wangli knew enough that of her own volition she immediately added. "Can't you come down? Now?"

"No."

Through Yuying, Xiao-an said that she'll be gone in a week, for the entire winter, to visit her brother in Ulaanbaatar, and won't be back until the spring festival.

And Wangli will be gone then too, back to his remote work unit in his alpine province. A pause followed, three *now-whats* eating away, creating their own space, until Xian-an said, "I'll never see you again," which didn't need any translating, her voice firm with resolution, everyone understanding very clearly that she meant every word of what she said and will now disappear from their lives completely.

"Tell her I'm sad; but I also understand," Wangli said, and then carelessly added, "Maybe there'll be another time this week before we both have to leave," everyone listening knowing that there would not be that, that there would not be the need for that either.

As Wangli walked the four flights up to the afternoon session for which he was the main presenter, he tripped over a step and fell flat-faced on the first landing. A custodian saw him slowly getting back up as if he were falling down again, one hand over his recent heart.

Counting

On October 1, 1949, when photographers were busily taking histori-
cal pictures of Mao Zedong proclaiming the creation of the People's
Republic of China atop the reviewing stands in Beijing's Tiananmen
Square, Professor Li Weibin, Mao's confidant and trusted advisor, was
standing by his side. You can see him in his long coat and glasses in the
photographs that were shot from the west.

Last month I interviewed him in his home in the Fragrant Hills
outside Beijing, the same location that prompted much of Cao Xuegin's
Dream of the Red Chamber. More than ninety years old by most ac-
counts, Professor Li was collected, lucid and did not make a single er-
ror of time, place or identity.

The visit extended over the entire weekend, and as he and his
granddaughter bade their farewells at the gates on Sunday evening, he
confided to me his wish to see his story published as soon as possible.

— Author's note

As often as Li told Mao to be careful, the head librarian would
always find out, if not today, then tomorrow, or the day after,
and without warning, she would emerge from behind a stack or
cart and the two of them would have to answer her same question
repeated again and again: "Why are you here, to work or read?" "If
you just want to read, go home and read." "Think, think, why are
you here?" No answer was acceptable — she was the assistant librarian. After the two of them were caught in the modern history
section for the third time in as many days, both Mao and Li were

sacked from their library jobs, thus ending their formal education at Beida. "You must remember we were very young then," Professor Li reminded me almost exactly seventy years later, "over there, there," pointing his walking cane towards the city without looking.

So out of the students' dormitory, the two of them carried all their belongings, bedrolls on their backs, some clothes, their *fanhes,* but mostly books secreted out of the library in their imaginations, and went into the streets that early May, 1919, looking for a place to stay. Some friends took them in, after they promised not to hold any secret meetings, a rigidly enforced covenant that was beginning to see some arrests and then disappearances.

Li knew it was doubtful the two of them would stay there long, but they were determined, not wanting to involve their friends in something irreversible. In fact, after the first two days, Li and Mao never returned, leaving everything, everything except their chance.

Our teacups were shaking on the table. At first I thought Professor Li had hit a leg of the table with his cane again.

"Tremors, just tremors," he said. "It happens here a lot."

But in 1900 there was more, but more was not enough, so that it shook again in 1911, 1919, 1928 and 1966. Now his granddaughter counted by his side, though he could well do it himself, his count still reliable. A doctor of the heart, she had requested a work-unit transfer here to be close to her grandfather. What she counted was entirely different, if she counted at all, that she allowed me to see in her eyes just once on the second day of the interview.

After 1919, Li and Mao separated, occasionally reappearing together in the most unusual places. When Mao took his arduous hike to Shaanxi Province in the winter of 1935, Li welcomed him at Yan'an and invited him to his son's wedding. On a flight over the Hump in 1944, a Flying Tiger pilot saw the two of them huddled together in the cargo hold, planning strategy amidst the filing cabinets and Steinway CD he was hauling around China for Madame Chiang just one gas tank ahead of her imminent defection.

"What was he like? What was old *huxi dai you suan wei* like, standing there on that autumn afternoon at the Gate of Heavenly Peace?"

His close friends and trusted theoreticians called him "garlic breath," his doctors advised him to quit smoking, and one warm night that summer, he personally rode around the capital putting his initials on every one of its forty-nine trolleys and five buses. But on October 1, 1949, nothing else seemed to matter. He was a monument there, facing south in the tumultuous afternoon sunlight, the city thronging with a million red and yellow chrysanthemums. Li and his son were with him, standing to his right, sharing his limelight, but they all knew the work had just begun.

"I was born next year," Professor Li's granddaughter added, her only words within my hearing that weekend.

Yes, and she would have been baptized by the bishop at Nantang if the Vatican had not ordered the Chinese Catholics to stop reading Chinese newspapers and wearing red scarves, red scarves, 1966, under red banners, there suddenly appeared at Beida's south gate, teenagers all, storming the gatekeepers, chanting, grabbing the head librarian by her hair and beating her to death, along with Professor Li's only son.

Yes, his granddaughter was in the middle of high school that year, and some of her classmates were responsible. Nevertheless she blamed Mao for doing nothing, and in two years went away to medical school to study what there was left of any healing.

There were no benches, count them, he said, there were no benches, not one, not a single one.

We sat there counting, one empty space after another in the photograph.

Baby, come hug, come hug and say goodbye.

Goodbye and come say baby, hug baby.

It reminded her of the night her father died. As she bent down to kiss him this last time, there was no smell of tobacco on his breath, on the night he died.

Come baby, come hug.

Sometimes our nerves are like that, brought about by our own carelessness, ignoring storm warnings, plain forgetting, or just looking the other way for no reason at all.

"What did you think, what did you think though as you stood there next to him with your son who would soon father a daughter and then be beaten to death by her classmates before she finished high school?"

There were no benches in sight, that is to say, there were no benches. Everyone was standing up, shouting, waving tiny red flags. It's true, RKO NEWS was there, recording it all. Edward Murrow too, but he didn't see any benches either. Even if he had seen any, he would not have mentioned it in his broadcast, since nobody in the United States would have believed him.

"So why were you counting benches when you knew there weren't any on the review stands or in the square that you couldn't see anyway?"

In the past perfect tense of Chinese grammar, he suggested that while he stood there between old garlic breath and his own son, he had anticipated this inevitable calamity. There is no other way to translate this.

What brought us back could have been anything, the grand-daughter getting up to replenish our tea, a tree in the courtyard shimmering in the light, anything at all. Who was to say why the breathing stopped, if it had stopped at all? Why were our voices filled with double meanings?

You know, he was always afraid of the cold, Professor Li added.

Yes, we know, though sometimes not by name, yes.

Baby, come, come say hug, come say goodbye.

The heart is such an extravagant organ.

Shapes

Ge thought he knew exactly what he was doing, finished the last sentence of the review for the Sunday issue with the line *Yuan wu zhan ye!,* and dropped off its only copy for the printer in the outgoing mail before heading out for a walk in the blustery evening to wait. With the government's post-Tiananmen Square encouragement of cultural opennness, the performance of Bizet's *Carmen* tonight with a cast from the National Conservatory of Music was nothing less than an international disaster, and Ge said so in his review — a faked Spanish opera performed in China and sung in French. Never mind what world opinion is, never mind what local opinion is — that Bizet had successfully managed to pawn off his *Carmen* as Spanish music since 1875.

His long walk took him to the other side of the city, and at two in the morning, he knocked on the door of his wife's apartment. Xiao-an was pursuing her own hectic career as a television producer and was not expecting him until the weekend. Heating up some water for tea and slightly irritated that Ge had not called first, she brushed her hair back and quickly removed the remains from her late snack before sitting down with him.

"What's wrong," she asked, her first words since opening the door.

"I bashed the *Carmen* production and mailed it," Ge said.

"You didn't. We love our opera. You're going to lose your job. You didn't." Xiao-an sighed.

"But I know. Even in our worst censorship years under Jiang Qing we produced Western operas in the Capital Theatre. You remember that last performance in the spring of 1966 just before everything collapsed."

"Before we were married? Yes, but that was different. There's nothing politically threatening in an eight-hour ring cycle about the filial entanglements of a mentally deficient and impulsive child. Everyone fell asleep, on both nights. For *Carmen* they brought back our famous singer from Paris."

While Xiao-an got up to make tea, Ge continued. "So I'll probably lose the review-*yuan,* but I just couldn't let this production get away with it. I've done that for too many years. I'm tired of it."

"Yes I know, I've seen you grow more indifferent about it recently. I hope my work doesn't take a turn. So far I've been allowed to do what I want, within reason, but no woman's been here before."

"How's your yurt project going?"

"I have the go-ahead. I leave for Ulaanbaatar with the camera crew next week."

"It'll be very cold."

"Yes, but the colors will be perfect. It's also very late. Will you stay?"

"No, I need the walk."

"You didn't come on your bicycle? You must stay, it's so late."

"No, I think I must go."

As she lingered at the door, Xiao-an smiled and added, "Don't worry, this way they won't ask you to review *Bolero.*"

—

Two days later the editor called Ge. He wasn't very happy about the review, but said he'd run it unchanged.

"Good, you just watch the typos," Ge said.

"Yes, and I hope the ceiling will not fall down on us."

"Unless I'm confused, the ceiling has fallen on them," Ge corrected.

"You better watch your mouth, you think you're protected being a professor at Beida?"

"I have tenure."

"Everyone in China has tenure. You think you're so different?"

"No, my friend, I'm just tired of minding what others are thinking. I'm tired of paying attention to politics every minute of every day and every night as if there is nothing else in life."

"All right, all right. I only called because I thought you might think we wouldn't print your piece. I didn't need a pamphlet; I read yours already, and wet my pants doing it. Listen, Ge, maybe you should emigrate to the United States in a Boeing 747 where you'll be welcomed as a dissident scholar and get to meet President Bush and Billy Graham on television."

"Look who's got the mouth now. At least that's something."

"And yours, asking their lives be spared, very funny. You better not go to the music school anymore — they've got a hit squad out after you."

"Maybe I should go there and get it over with. That way I won't have to keep looking over my shoulder for someone to whack me."

"Ge, you're too much, and you'll be punished."

"You too, and thanks for the call."

Ge stood by the phone looking into it for a minute before calling Xiao-an at her studio.

"Xiao-an, it's Friday."

"Yes I know. What are you doing?"

"How about dinner tonight?"

"I can't, I have a meeting. Is something wrong?"

"No, no matter, it was just an impulse. See you tomorrow."

After he hung up the phone, Ge sat down and lit a cigarette, blowing its smoke into the afternoon sunlight. He looked at the stack of his unfinished articles on his table and wondered if he dared to finish them. One of them mentioned Dolly Parton and Lenin in the same sentence. He thought he'd be the first to admit what little it took to turn a thing around, but also what little it took to make a thing go all wrong.

—

These thoughts crowded his interior space in his evening walk. He could not understand why his office building that's already walled-in within a walled-out campus with guards, was locked down tight at eleven every night, with no one but the janitor and department leader allowed a key; and he could not understand why the building was opened on holidays, but his personal office with the computer, sealed by a piece of paper, its script forbidding entrance. Just this morning one of his graduate students told him that the campus security office had held a policy meeting and decided that the dormitories would be locked down every night between eleven and midnight, to discourage vandalism and theft, when there has been no theft, when there had been no vandalism. These were the little disturbances that made things go wrong, these terribly simple acts that were meticulously planned and diligently, enthusiastically and patriotically carried out by good people, with malice toward none.

Ge thought that against this populist tradition of forty centuries, it was a miracle what Mao and Zhou and now Deng and Li have changed in China, particularly in the face of pressing external mercantile impatience. He could see the same kind of impatience in some of his graduate students, some of whom he had suspected of being Tiananmen Square activists he had defended, some of whom were outright materialistic and only wanted to live a different illusionary life in the United States or Australia, who will first ace the TOEFL test and then leave one at a time, sometimes abandoning husbands or wives or children with indifference, changing their mainland shapes.

When Ge took the diagonal that led to the forestry school, he could see even in the dark that things were different. The shapes of buildings and high-rise apartments disappeared; instead the few buildings were small on one side of the street, and on the other, the land still dominated by tract-farming, in this old neighborhood that hadn't yet exactly modernized in Beijing's annexation plans. A young couple bicycled towards him, laughing. Three old men gathered at a pedlar's late stand were smoking and gossiping madly. Ge wanted to stop and visit with them, but he knew it would not be possible, his motives would not be expected. So he took the long loop around the universities, hands in pocket, before heading back to his Beida apartment.

A phone message from Xiao-an was waiting for him, *Meeting cancelled, dinner tonight?* A little impulsive for her, Ge thought, for someone who's normally very cautious and dedicated to changing only one thing at a time. When they first met, they were drawn to each other in common grief in their last year in middle-school when their fathers were both beaten to death on the same night by the Red Guards. Two years later they escaped this shared understanding of their world by getting married before college. And now, some twenty years later, their marriage held together by scheduling imperatives, like those of his colleagues and friends who also got married during that period of upheaval, he wondered if something else had happened, if Xiao-an had something pressing to tell him.

—

They ordered their food deliberately. From the way Xiao-an sat back from the table, Ge knew something was approaching.

"Ge, I've been thinking."

"Xiao-an?"

"We've been married since the end of middle-school, twenty years exactly."

"Yes, dutifully committed, lifelong partners."

"But we're so watchful of everything that we don't feel anything."

"That's true Xiao-an, but we're mature adults, not impulsive school kids mooning."

"But that's it exactly," Xiao-an paused while the waitress set down the first dish. "We have never been school kids in love. You know what I'm talking about, yet the two of us can sit here and discuss it as calmly as if we were talking about joining a VCR club.

That's not a marriage, that makes marriage not even a symbol of anything, anything at all."

"Yes, that's true."

"It's more a mask."

"That's true too," Ge said, picking up his chopsticks and wiping them clean with a piece of paper from his pocket.

"Or an illusion."

"That too."

"Don't you see you are agreeing with me on everything, Ge? We are so equal we each have our own apartment. It's disgusting, and a waste. That's not marriage."

"Are you suggesting we shack up again?"

"That's not even funny Ge."

"No, but you're more emotional about this than you're willing to admit. You haven't even picked up your chopsticks."

"Ge, listen. Don't you see us? Don't you see what's happening?"

Ge set down his chopsticks and looked away. He wanted to light a cigarette, but wished at this moment that he didn't smoke.

"Xiao-an, I know exactly what you're talking about. It's the same all over China, don't you see that's what marriage has become, my good friend?"

"If that's what it is, then I want a divorce," Xiao-an said, picking up her chopsticks.

"I know, but it will restrict your career."

"I'm willing to take the risk." Xiao-an looked down, rearranging her chopsticks carefully on her plate.

"You'll not see me anymore."

"You're full of wolf dung. That's not true, you're my best friend."

"You'll not sleep with me anymore."

"The way we do it, it is no matter."

"It's a good thing we don't have children" Ge said and started laughing, and then choking.

"You mean *one* child. Yes, it's a good thing, I don't want to be a breeding machine for the state, spoil the child crazy with affection until the state takes over at the propaganda age."

"Be careful Xiao-an, they're listening behind you," Ge said, picking up his chopsticks and waving them at the couple behind her.

"There's nothing new for them here. But if it'll make you feel any better, we can speak in English, if you wish, or we can put our heads down and produce some tears for their entertainment."

"*Bu shi.* And you'll still go to Ulaanbaatar next week?"

"Oh you romantic fool, of course, nothing's changed."

"That's what you think. Tell me, Xiao-an, do you feel betrayed?"

"By what? Knowing what it was, we ran and couldn't wait to get ourselves into it."

"But now you want more? Hah!"

"No, Ge, I want less, that's why I want a divorce," Xiao-an said, and her gaze would not let go.

So the two of them sat there, looking at the change, occasionally taking a small bite, waiting, and waiting.

At last Xiao-an sighed, and didn't want anymore. They both looked at the same window. Out in the street an old woman was riding a trailer-bicycle loaded more than ten-feet high with flattened cardboard. She was pressing down on the pedals hard, and then harder still, while other cyclists passed her on both sides in the semi-dark. Behind her, an old man was running and pushing the trailer with both hands. He was also looking down as he ran. Someone appeared and waved at all of them, a pair of castanets shaking in the background, the bamboo curtain in the restaurant clinking in the slight breeze. Moving ever so slowly, the couple passed, and then disappeared entirely. Xiao-an and Ge could hear someone yelling from the back of the kitchen.

Unmovable Things

Your life is bound to be different when your mother is a doctor. What do I remember about this? Slight in build, Lao Ma is always ready to side with the weak and the sick. Often seeing more than one hundred patients a day at the clinic, she would nevertheless give her time to inquire about their families and home provinces. Always holistic in her approach to healing, she would sometimes write letters on their behalf to agencies or officials, complaining of a cruel and corrupt landlord, or searching for a relative who had disappeared in the late sixties.

Lao Ma was equally diligent and dedicated at home, which in itself is frightening. Though the closest she had come to cooking anything was boiling a beaker of water in high-school chemistry, she would determine our weekly menus and detail the foods we were to avoid, a bulletin board cycling the seasonal diseases, typhoid, cholera, hepatitis *yi* and *er,* the Seattle flu. And it seemed to work. When we were all living at home, no one ever contracted a contagious disease or got seriously ill, although my baby sister Xiao-mi caught malaria on a camping trip, little brother Xiao-shi acquired the irritating pastime of reading in the bathroom from the stacks of the American magazine *Reader's Digest* that were stored there, and Old Guo sometimes drank too much, but Lao Ma sure put an end to that one day when she poured all of his imported brandy down a sink.

So far as these things were concerned, things were okay at home. We did not smoke, play mahjong, or get sick, and the children always studied hard, Xiao-mi taking a slide of her *plasmodium vivax* to her biology class for extra credit, and especially Xiao-shi, memorizing all the country jokes and the biographies of all the unforgettable persons on earth, but to this day would not tell us what else he learned in that bathroom. Our social life was something else however.

Ever conscious of the family cohesion, Lao Ma would organize various family outings, a trip to the western lakes in warm weather, an opera matinee when Peili was in town, but it was the occasional dinners out that I quickly learned to dread. Lao Ma always carried a bottle of rubbing alcohol with her, and would produce it from her purse at the restaurant table, carefully spilling a liberal quantity onto the cotton balls she had also brought along for this purpose, wiping clean each place setting passed around the table to her. I think this dramatic display of sanitization was an embarrassment to everyone else at the table, but Lao Guo and Xiao-shi said nothing, while Xiao-mi and I argued for all of us. We've had shots and inoculations every other week, we're in a clean restaurant, you would not take us into a dirty restaurant would you, cholera is not on the bulletin board this month, we'll taste the lingering stench of alcohol on our chopsticks and on our food too; but nothing ever changed her mind, her precautionary Methodist sterilization procedure always prevailed.

We soon learned to join the weak and avoid the sick, at least Xiao-mi and I did, and let Lao Ma represent our gourmet interests, especially when one of Xiao-mi's classmates saw us performing our family ritual and later whispered it to everyone at the next recess. Since then we have tried to get it over with as quickly as possible, to maintain our dignity along with the lumps, with Xiao-mi persistently ducking her head under the table pretending to retie a shoelace or retrieve a hairpin.

The children have moved away and Lao Ma is retired now, and though we are not weak or sick, she would visit us once in a while, Xiao-mi more than me, probably because she is her daughter and they live in the same province. She never visits Xiao-shi, though it is perhaps because he does not want her to, I am not sure, though I still suspect he learned something important sitting in that *cue-suo* that the rest of the children can only guess. Before her visits she would always send a note telling me what time her train would arrive, what track it would be on and reminding me to meet her at her car on time because she is too slight to lift her bags. Xiao-mi has told me that she gets these notes too, in the same indecipherable handwriting that we have learned to understand through the years, still using the same kind of notepaper advertising the newest foreign pharmaceutical discoveries, a lifelong supply of Abbott, Lilly, Squibb, and Parke-Davis. None of us are weak or sick, that much I am thankful for.

The Burning

He did not care about going to work this morning, he had been attacked by strange dreams last night. To rid himself of the ambiguous messages that had invaded his sleep, he repeated to himself *When does something become nothing at all*, while maneuvering his bicycle over two inches of snow that had also fallen in the night, a tricky challenge to survival.

Perhaps it had started when he wasn't paying any particular attention, half dozing, absorbing one tv commercial after another before finally gathering enough stamina to turn off the set, perhaps too late then, having already been seduced along with half the families in China by its lurid images of refrigerators, hair shampoo and washing machines. Perhaps it was the *Hehua* washing machine that did it, scrambling Zhang's sense of time and space enough that invited his nightmares. Set in a remote village in distant Shaanxi Province, it showed a group of women hand-washing clothes in large wooden buckets by the edge of a gurgling brook, lazily chatting in the tranquil sunshine, perhaps speculating about astronomy, illusions and when electricity will come to their rural village. A mustard Toyota pickup truck in four-wheel drive pulled up and delivered a limegreen washing machine, and Zhang remembered guessing that even if it'll only rust in someone's shed for months or even years, it'll just be a matter of time and enough marriages before history will find its way there, along with the dy-

namo and coiled copper wire to make the automatic washer shake
and spin.

At the hotel where he worked, Zhang went about inspecting
the rooms automatically, even after his supervisor had reminded
him that this was a burn-day. Still distracted by his dreams and in
his indifference to the hotel's joint-ventured owners who lived in
Kuwait, Paris, Tokyo and Hong Kong and whom he had never met
nor seen a picture of, Zhang mindlessly made the counts and sev-
enteen-point inspection. The only item today for the burn-pile
was found in the closet in 307, an out-of season Liz Claiborne
dress in a plastic garment bag, which he carried with him for the
rest of his rounds, half thinking that it was perhaps just the perfect
size for his mother.

The official policy demanded that clothes left by foreigners in
all the hotels must be burned, thus lessening the spread of com-
municable diseases against which the residents have no immunity.
Zhang had thought that this was feudal and bizarre, but knowing
the futility, as well as the risk of challenging a government directive, he had always obeyed, even though privately he continued to
think that with a good working washing machine and all the
clothes the foreigners leave in order to make room in their luggage
for their Beijing bargain purchases, thousands of the poor and
homeless could be dressed in the latest western fashion. So too this
time, he numbly took the dress and the garment bag and threw
them onto the pile by the outside burn-barrel, where a small
crowd of hotel workers had gathered in the fresh snow in front of
the CCTV camera crew.

The dumbbell resident manager started using his bamboo stick
to lift the clothing articles one-by-one into the barrel, conspicu-

ously smiling for the television camera. Zhang recognized the overcoat left by Reisa Gorbachev in favor of a local mink, four Elton John's hats, and some purple bras and panties that he could not be sure as belonging to Linda Rondstat or Henry Kissinger's travelling companion. Someone from heating had brought up a can of petrol, which he liberally poured onto the clothes when the barrel was half full, and the Dumbbell, still wearing his It's Me expression for the camera, stood back and threw another match into the barrel, after missing with the first two. The crowd's gasps rose as suddenly as the instantly exploding flare of the flames, turning to *Ahs* and *Sighs* when the fire burned into different colors as the synthetic fabrics reached their respective combustible levels, sometimes green, sometimes magenta, and sometimes yellow and rose, witnessing a miniature fireworks display, a kaleidoscope gone wild and bursting out of its tube.

Zhang left the crowd and went inside into the administrative lounge, where he sat down and thought about his life, if only he could change it, or some of its parts, or understand the meaning of his dreams. He dismissed the possibility of a transfer to another hotel, going abroad was hopeless, and going back to school for retraining was also out of the question. He reached into his pocket and found no more than six *yuan*, he added. He then had an idea, that if he could save ten *yuan* a week, in a year or so he would have enough for a Lotus Flower automatic washer, and with that he could start recycling the leftover clothes, anonymously giving them away to the needy. With a wry smile on his face, he got up and left a two *yuan* note on a nearby table, a small payment for his new life of disobedience and the spots that cannot be removed.

Lipstick

TODAY:

This man is serious. He has put a map of the Mall in my hands and is now insisting that after meeting with the media at the Washington Monument the parade/demonstration must be routed to the White House for a final statement.

"You're crazy," I shout above the other voices, a strategy I learned at Columbia's democracy salon. "We'll need two permits. One from the Park Service for the Mall maybe, but the city will never give us one for Pennsylvania Avenue on the same day. Impossible."

Wang shakes his sheen of shoulder-length hair from side to side, practicing for the tv cameras. It glistens in the subdued light of the living room. It's gorgeous and its image has already been beamed to every TV set on both sides of the Pacific. Then abruptly he looks straight at me, his seriousness and sincerity focused for the photo-journalist's close up.

"Look, we're all here," Wang sweeps his arm around the crowded apartment. "Even double-exiled Black Cat from San Diego."

"We know, we know," yells someone from the kitchen. "Where he's been selling Yamaha guitars after his expulsion from Berkeley for lying about his Green Card. YA-MA-HA. Ha, ha, good thing

171

he lives in California. For penance he must offer his Nanjing grandmother oranges every week."

"We must be serious here," Wang continues, Wang the career organizer, who has put this curious coalition together, COC, Committee of Overseas Chinese, ever watchful of human rights violations in China and always promoting the struggle for democracy in the motherland.

But what he says is true, we're all here, half of Beijing's leaders' children all gathered in one room in America, the third brain drain this century — Qing from Brandeis who still sleeps with the lights on, Gao holding down a Nieman at Harvard, Liu from CUNY, and even crazy Li from Michigan State. A casually tossed grenade here can seriously alter China's future.

"We must also select someone to make the speech," that same voice yells from the kitchen.

"What about the physicist Fang Lizhi?" Xiao Liu raises her hand. She is rumored to be dating an American, but she has not changed her Beijing-styled bobbed-hair.

"No, that won't work," Wang answers. "Nobody trusts a physicist, not since Galileo."

"He wasn't a physicist, you idiot," Black Cat shudders. "But I agree with you. Fang's not very good in front of a camera, in either language, Chinese or English, physics or politics."

Here comes the silence of agreement, the vast stillness of conspiracy hatched some ten years ago in Beijing, before the first gathering in front of the Gate of Heavenly Peace in April.

"We need someone younger, someone with good teeth, someone who'll make those mothers in Peoria cry over their TV dinners and send us their checks before their husbands come home," Xiao

Liu volunteers. Ever the consensus builder, she has not yet abandoned her role of saying what everyone else in the room is already thinking.

"All right then. What about Wang Dan?" Someone had to say it, and it is Black Cat. "He's recognizable, even for America's short memory. Good in front of cameras, and he sounds convincing with his new dentures. He even mentions those prisoners that have been left behind — surely that will wring some hearts for our cause."

"Yeah, but there's always that rogue reporter out there who's going to make him slip, even with an interpreter. It happened twice last year, in Milwaukee and in Denver." Wang sounds very sure of himself — he has stopped shaking his hair for this announcement. "He's going to be our next president; we can't expose him to any negative publicity."

"What about that student who stopped the tanks during the demonstration at Tiananmen Square?" asks Simon Fraser's Chen, a wannabe from the south who speaks a passable Mandarin but has been accepted because of his success at raising funds from Hong Kong's motherland candle burners.

"You mean Charlie Cole's *Newsweek* photo that's reprinted all over the world a hundred times every June 4?" Black Cat asks between sucks on his funky cigarettes. "I thought everyone knew he didn't stop those tanks of the 38th Army in T-Square — those four tanks were unarmed, and they stopped for him. It isn't just a squabble between interpretations. I thought everyone knew that. Strange that we've never been able to identify him. Perhaps he was a MSS agent."

Alex Kuo

"Or he was a student swiftly arrested and imprisoned," Chen argues.

"All right you two, all right," Wang intercedes, shaking his hair. "Let's not fight among ourselves. We still have a lot to decide before meeting with the Park Service tomorrow."

"Hey, let's order out some Chinese," that same person yells from the kitchen. "That'll get some work done."

TOMORROW:

Date: *October 10*
Time: *9:00 A.M. for staging*
10:00 A.M. to 12:00 for parade, up Independence Avenue to Washington Monument

Wang, Black Cat, Xiao Liu and I are at the Park Service office filling out a form for a parade/demonstration permit. We have been here for more than an hour, and are having some problems with these questions.

Organization: *COC*
Address:
Officers:

"Looks like you could do with some friendly assistance with that form," a woman's voice drifts to us from the blind side. A ranger with shorter hair than Xiao Liu's has come to help.

"Yes. Thanks, ma'am," Wang turns around, shaking his hair.

174

"Please don't mam me," the ranger says. "I'm here to help, and my name is Dorene Okamura," she smiles, patting her burnished name plate over her starched left pocket.

Wang looks at me, but I pretend not to know what his look means. Instead I hand Dorene Okamura the form and the Park Service pen.

"This is as far as we've come," I add.

"The Washington Monument, that's okay, Fifteenth and Constitution, still within the Mall," Dorene Okamura reads the form. "Let's see here. Okay so far. Hmmmmmm."

Xiao Liu is beaming with admiration.

"October 10. Hmmm. That might be a problem," Dorene Okamura looks at me. "Another group has also applied for a permit for the same time that day. Perhaps you know? Human Rights Watch, Human Rights in China, and AI?"

"We didn't know." It is Wang who answers.

Ranger Okamura continues to talk to me, as if my running shoes, baseball hat and no cloud of tobacco stink encircling me make me less likely to misunderstand her words.

"But we can work it out," she says. "They'll be going up Constitution Avenue. Would you have any problems if the two groups saw each other four blocks apart?"

She is directing the question to me again, but it is Wang who answers, again.

"No problem," he says, in the same tone of voice as if the ranger had just changed her order from a Big Mac to a Double Cheeseburger. "Who's their speaker?" he asks.

"I think Were Kaiser, but I'm not sure."

"Yes, you mean Wu'er Kaixi, that Uighur minority hooligan from Beijing Normal, that exploiter of human tragedy? I thought he was in Australia or Japan, last I heard."

"Wherever," Dorene Okamura says. "But they said he'll be here October 10. 10:45 A.M. The media's been prompted. My job is to see to three things: first that there'll be no conflict between the two parades; then ensure the media will have appropriate access to both groups in an orderly manner; and make sure there will be enough port-o-potties for everyone. We also provide the necessary deputized security to make sure these things will happen, and in the right order."

I can tell that Xiao Liu wants to know what a *port-o-potty* is, but she looks down at the floor tiling instead, suppressing the question for later.

"These demonstration plans look pretty controlled and re-hearsed to me," Black Cat speaks for the first time. "Whatever happened to good ol' spontaneous demonstration?"

"We don't believe there's ever been a spontaneous demonstration in human history." Ranger Okamura looks ready for the cameras. "Not even in front of the Hilton in 1968 Chicago. In Indonesia last year, first a truck shows up with the demonstrators, then a minute later another truck loaded with rocks. They are all planned, some more successfully than others."

"If any of your people plan on being at high places," she adds, "such as roof tops, monuments or trees, we must know where and their names."

The four of us take turns looking at each other and say nothing.

The ranger continues.

"There'll be a staging area available to you at nine," she walks to the wall map and points to a small section off the freeway at the junction of Independence and Third. "Here you can organize your pro-democracy parade. Are you sure you don't know about the other group?" She looks straight at Wang who is busily shaking his hair, which has become his answer to everything he wants to avoid.

Black Cat and I exchange looks to say nothing, and it is Xiao Liu who answers the ranger.

"Yes, at the staging area we can put on makeup for the cameras. Some powder so our faces won't shine under the bright lights. Some lipstick too. We must look young, energetic and dedicated to democracy."

The rest of the details are worked out quickly with the efficient ranger. Just as quickly I lose interest in this meeting, so Dorene Okamura is talking directly to Wang instead.

SOMETIME LATER:

My mind wanders back to the Beijing of ten years ago. We did it wrong back then, and we're doing it wrong again on this side of the Pacific. It's now beginning to be doubtful that we're ever going to survive the messiness of this part of our history.

But when the meeting is over, I will drive to the Georgetown Mall to look for just the right shade of Revlon. I will find the exact lipstick that will let everyone in the world know just enough, not too much, and not too little. Maybe a *Cappuccino* or *Natural Nude* that won't kiss off. So they will have no doubts. So they will continue to believe.

Exit, A Chinese Novel

No one has been to Beijing
Without a visit to Tiananmen.

— from a tourist brochure

Crazy Shu wrote these harmless lines forty years ago at the end of the war, when he was yet a teenager. It was October 1, still wearing the remnants of a soldier's uniform and drenched in tears of hope in Tiananmen Square, he stood under the yellow and red banners surrounding Mao Zedong's proclamation of a new nation. Then a young poet from Ruili Province, he could have said the same thing about a visit to his Ruili River. But this was 1949, and Chiang Kaishek had just fled to Taiwan with all of China's gold reserves and Steinway CDs.

Two years later Crazy Shu became Mao's special aide, traversing the country giving poetry readings and encouraging younger writers, occasionally arbitrating canonical disputes among scholars and party officials. At his very last meeting with Mao in early 1976, Mao glued a poem to his heart: *If the world is round, then everything will eventually come to the same point.*

Crazy Shu never married, but hung on to all his things, both new and broken. After Mao's death, he was appointed a deputy to the Ministry of Broadcasting, Film and Media, and assigned as principal speech writer for select members of the party's central committee. His mental notes accumulated between the lines of these printed speeches while he ignored their public reading — a disgruntled literacy against the state-owned telecaster echoing the number of words in each utterance and counting those in attendance for the evening's local news. Secretly he did not believe that these hyper-real speeches would change anyone's mind, even if they were required reading at the mandatory weekly political study meetings at all levels in the nation. As the leader of his department, he was aware that as much as his writers wanted to, they could not believe what they had written. On those occasions when he visited some factories in Beijing to see how these speeches were being received, he noticed that the fastest readers had been selected to read them to a post-lunch audience half dozing and half reading something else tucked down in front of them. After one such visit during which he saw that the party reader was reading from the factory's WWII evacuation manual since the printed speech had not arrived on time, he contemplated starting a rumor that would eliminate these meetings.

But in fact, after the Tiananmen Square incident this year, these required meetings doubled. Crazy Shu was in the western provinces during the spring, and did not hear of the event until his return in late June. As he was being driven back and forth on Chang-gan Boulevard to learn what he could from the intervals between the recently-scrubbed stones, he was tempted to ask the driver to stop and let him out. But school children and tourists from Shanghai and Japan were there posing for pictures between the lions at Tiananmen Square, the Gate of Heavenly Peace, so he thought better of disturbing their play and privacy for the sake of what by now was perhaps nothing more than empty curiosity.

Instead, he thought there comes a time when something happens that so totally devastates one's perceptions of hope, belief and act, that instinctively and personally one knows that he cannot live like that in that country anymore. He remembered his commemorative poem about the successful revolution forty years ago, and how free of censors he had felt in writing it. But in these recent years he has come to believe that poetry held too much shelter for misfired metaphors and indulgent lies, and that, that is the real toad. Even with censors and informants all around him, he was beginning to believe that fiction can better get at the exposed nerve, however elusive. This time, not trusting poetry anymore, he defected into the beginning of his first story:

If you forgot who you are, or do not recognize yourself in your photos, you can look at their numbers. One survives by realizing that you can re-imagine it. So Crazy Shu pretended to take the Ministry's next assignment in Stockholm, but already he was doubting that he could change anything leading the life of a refugee, a DP. What can he do with his spare time besides get up every morning and try to survive the day? *Tell me!* he pleaded with himself. Learn to play a rueful violin and look for a quartet to play with every Thursday evening? Give poetry readings as a dissident writer and rely on the generosity of PEN International? String for the CIA or Mossad?

At Shanghai where passports and exit visas were checked for the last time, Crazy Shu thought he recognized an odor on the airport concourse as something familiar from his Ruili childhood, but he wasn't sure it wasn't just unfinished presswood from another past or his imagination. From Hong Kong's Kai Tak airport, foreign faces started appearing in his British Airways 747. Some read the Bible for the first time, and some listened to a Romanian student who was at the Palace Square say, "I do not believe in good or bad communists, just communists. They are all crooks."

Now Crazy Shu put away the story he was writing, and looked out the cabin window from 30,000 feet. Remembering the exiled Cubans in Miami and Chinese in Taiwan, he thought that symbolic expatriation was seldom an option, and effective even less often — though it mattered more to him that he had never been given the chance to give the heart of his heart, than that the rest of his life might be worse than what he was leaving behind — and wondered if the real China will ever stand up.

Orchid Pavilion Books

Orchid Pavilion Books is the literary imprint of Asia 2000 Ltd., Hong Kong publishers of quality books since 1980. The imprint is inspired by the *Orchid Pavilion Preface*, a treatise on life penned by Wang Xizhi, China's most famous calligrapher.

To quote from *Behind the Brushstrokes*, an Asia 2000 book by Khoo Seow Haw and Nancy Penrose:

> By 352 A.D., Wang Zizhi was 50 years old, his reputation as a calligrapher was well established, and he had served as a court minister for many years. In the late spring of that year Wang Xizhi invited 41 calligraphers, poets, relatives and friends to accompany him on an outing to Lan Ting, the Orchid Pavilion, in the city of Shaoxing, Zhejiang province. It was the time of the year for the purification ceremony, when hands and bodies were cleansed with stream water to wash away any bad luck. The group of friends and scholars sat on each side of a flowing stream, and a little cup made out of a lotus leaf, full of wine, was floated down the stream. Whenever it floated in front of someone, that person was obliged to either compose a poem on the spot or to drink the wine as forfeit if he failed to come up with a poem.

> By the end of the day, 37 poems had been composed by 25 scholars. Wang Xizhi, as the head of this happy occasion, picked up a brush made out of rat whiskers and hairs and wrote on the spot the greatest masterpiece of Chinese calligraphy, the *Lan Ting Xu*, or the *Orchid Pavilion Preface*. Written on silk in the outstanding style of *Xing Shu* (Walking Style), the composition contains 28 vertical rows and 324 words. It is a philosophical discourse on the meaning of life. Wang Xizhi's calligraphy in this work is full of a natural energy, inspired by the happiness and grace of the moment, brimming with refinement and elegance. The *Orchid Pavilion Preface* became the greatest piece of *Xing Shu* and, although Wang Xizhi later tried more than 100 times to reproduce the work, he was never able to match the quality of the original.

Quality Books

Orchid Pavilion
Asia 2000 Ltd.

Fiction

A Change of Flag	Christopher New
Cheung Chau Dog Fanciers' Society	Alan B Pierce
Childhood's Journey	Wu Tien-tze
Chinese Opera	Alex Kuo
Connections – Stories of East Asia	David T. K. Wong
Dance with White Clouds	Goh Poh Seng
Getting to Lamma	Jan Alexander
Last Seen in Shanghai	Howard Turk
Lipstick and Other Stories	Alex Kuo
Riding a Tiger, The Self-Criticism of Arnold Fisher	Robert Abel
Sergeant Dickinson	Jerome Gold
Shanghai	Christopher New
Temutma	Rebecca Bradley & Stewart Sloan
The Chinese Box	Christopher New
The Ghost Locust	Heather Stroud
The Last Puppet Master	Stephen Rogers
The Mongolian Connection	Scott Christiansen

Poetry

An Amorphous Melody – A Symphony in Verse	Kavita
Coming Ashore Far From Home	Peter Stambler
New Ends, Old Beginnings	Louise Ho
Round – Poems and Photographs of Asia	Barbara Baker & Madeleine Slavick
Salt	Mani Rao
The Last Beach	Mani Rao
Traveling With a Bitter Melon	Leung Ping-kwan
Water Wood Pure Splendour	Agnes Lam
Woman to Woman	Agnes Lam

Order from Asia 2000 Ltd

15 B, 263 Hollywood Road, Sheung Wan, Hong Kong
Telephone: (852) 2530-1409; Fax: (852) 2526-1107
E-mail: sales@asia2000.com.hk; Website: http://www.asia2000.com.hk